MW00962477

KING HENRY'S CHOICE

EMILY-JANE HILLS ORFORD

Clean Reads

GREAT STORIES. NO GUILT.

www.cleanreads.com

King Henry's Choice
by Emily-Jane Hills Orford
Published by Clean Reads
www.cleanreads.com

PRAISE FOR QUEEN MARY'S DAUGHTER

This novel is a masterpiece, written by a great storyteller, one who leads readers into the workings of the hearts of her characters and allows them to explore the conflicts inherent to human nature.

... Romuald Dzemo, Readers' Favorite, readers-favorite.com

a highly original, fast-paced, skillfully written alternate history set in the sixteenth, seventeenth and twenty-first centuries.

*... **Ruth Latta**, author of "Grace in Love"*

Emily-Jane Hills Orford has the amazing capacity to weave a tale of intrigue, history and war that keeps the reader involved, entertained and absorbed.

... Phyllis Bohonis, author of "The Track"

To Gran
Margaret Murray Dickson Downer
(1902-1995)
a woman with a true Scottish heart
and a passion for what might have been
my mentor, my friend, my beloved grandmother
a woman who would truly appreciate my what if scenarios

ONE

Holyrood House, Edinburgh, Scotland, March 1ˢᵗ, Year of Our Lord 1649

"You're exhausted, Grandmother. You must rest."

"Rest is for those who lie six feet under, Henry. As soon I will be."

He reached across the table and gently took her hand in his, stroking the back with his thumbs. The room was dim; the glow from the hearth next to the table dwindled along with the flames. The morning light was barely filtering through the led-pained windows behind him. His eyes searched hers for answers she could not give, truths she could not know. He had to tell her. He knew he did. Would she believe him? Would it make any difference if she did believe him? Where does this truth lead him now? So many questions. So few answers.

The biggest question. Always. Why?

Why him?

Why this many great grandmother of his?

Why now?

Why later?

Why any time?

Time was irrelevant.

Time was obscure.

Time was of the essence.

But was time real?

And, if time was or wasn't real, why now?

Why?

Why?

Why?

"You know our days are numbered." Her voice pulled him out of his endless list of questions. Her smile soothed his soul. It didn't erase his questions though. It just soothed as a grandmother's smile often did. Warm and welcoming. Encouraging and full of love. She was his grandmother, many greats removed. A grandmother full of love.

"I am just about finished writing my story and I will place all of these journals in the secret compartment behind the stone over there." She pointed just beyond the hearth to the encasing of large grey stones collected from the rocky terrain that stretched across much of the Scottish landscape.

The task complete, the scratching of the quill against paper ceased. She closed the book and closed her eyes, whispering the concluding words by heart. Her mother's prayer. The words of the fated woman known as Mary Queen of Scots. "Keep us, Oh God, from pettiness; let us be large in thought, in word, in deed. Let us be done with fault-finding and leave off self-seeking. May we put away all pretense and meet each other, face to face, without self-pity and without prejudice. May we never be hasty in judgement and always generous. Let us take time for all things; make us to grow calm, serene, gentle. Teach us to put in action our better impulses: straight forward and unafraid. Granted, we may realize it is the little things of life which create difficulties and it is in these big things of life we are as one. Oh, Lord, let us not forget to be kind."

Silence followed. He broke it. In a firm, but soft voice, he uttered the battle cry of his country, the battle cry which had started with this great grandmother (many times removed).

"For now and forever." He paused and breathed deeply. "Grandmother." It was now or never. He had to tell her. She deserved to know the truth. "I have been to the future – way into the future. I have met them."

"Who, Henry? Met who?" Her voice was weakening.

"We have been used as guinea pigs, Grandmother. Lab rats." He wasn't reaching her. His voice was falling on deaf ears. He could tell. She was fading. Fast. It was obvious she didn't understand what he was talking about. He wanted her to know, though. He wanted to share with her what he had learned. He spoke quickly, hoping his words would reach her before it was too late. But what did it matter now? This knowledge he carried wouldn't follow her beyond the grave.

"Scientists in the twenty-fifth century have traveled through time and implanted tracing devices in our heads, like the microchips they started implanting in pets in the late twentieth century. We were the chosen. We were studied intently. We have been followed, stalked through time."

Noticing her eyes seeking something behind him, he shifted in his chair to look towards the window. Shadows of figures glimmered, slowly taking shape. There were three. They were all smiling at him and beckoning to his grandmother. When his eyes faced her again, she was slumped over. He felt for a pulse. There was none.

"For now and forever," he murmured as he allowed the tears to streak down his cheeks unchecked. "I will see you in the future, Grandmother. Nemo me impune lacessit. For now and forever."

TWO

Sometime in the Future, Somewhere Unrecognizable

He opened his eyes slowly. The glare of the overhead light struck mercilessly into his irises. He blinked rapidly and tried to raise one arm in order to cover his eyes. To protect them from the glare. He couldn't. Something was stopping his movement. He tried to move his legs. They were restrained as well.

He tried to lift his head, to turn his head, to look.

Nothing.

All he could do is look up.

At the light.

It glared unforgivingly into his eyes.

He opened his mouth to speak, to yell, to make some noise. His mouth seemed to open, but no sound came out.

A shadow approached.

"Ah!" A man in a white lab coat hovered over him, his magnifying goggles sliding down his nose, a stethoscope wrapped around his neck. "You're awake. Good. Now you must rest."

Strapped to a bed, with no voice, he valiantly tried again to speak. Nothing.

The man held up his hand. "No. You can't speak and you can't move, Your Majesty. For your own protection. You've just had another implant inserted. You won't remember. You're not supposed to remember. We hope this implant will help you forget better than the previous two."

Your Majesty. The man had offered him appropriate consideration. For what? He was confused. His name was Henry. It was starting to come back. The mind fog was lifting. King Henry I of Scotland. Yes. He was King Henry I. What was he doing here? In this medical-like facility with what appeared to be a doctor hovering over him? Why was he chained to the bed? Something to do with an implant. Another one? They hoped it would help him forget? Forget what?

"Why?" He managed to take control of his voice. It was more of a croak than the sound he was accustomed to hearing.

"You're in the year 2445, Your Majesty. Well into the future and a long way from your time. There are powers at play you just can't begin to understand, sir."

"Where?" All he could do was sputter.

"Holyrood House, Your Majesty. Your home."

"What is this implant? What is it?"

No answer.

"Answer me." He was becoming agitated. He was used to getting what he wanted. He was in charge. He was the king.

No answer.

"Why? Why? Why?" The recurring question. He had jumped around through time since he was a young boy and he had found himself in some rather interesting, and dangerous situations. But this was by far the most bizarre. 2445. It was well into the future. He couldn't remember a similar jump this far ahead in time. What did it all mean? Implants. Forgetting. He didn't want to forget. He wanted to remember. Everything.

No answer.

He felt a prick. Something sharp went into his arm and everything faded away.

THREE

Holyrood House, Edinburgh, May 1st, Year of Our Lord 1875

He awoke covered in sweat, his bedclothes and sheets tangled in a mess which had him somewhat pinned to the bed. Coming to full consciousness, he sat up with a start and took in his surroundings.

His bed. Draped with finely embroidered canopies and covered with soft wool blankets.

His room. Large, spacious, comfortable, with all his chosen furnishings in their correct place.

His window, complete with the aging leaded panes, left open slightly the way he liked it, a gentle breeze blowing in the scent of the heather bushes growing in the garden below.

"It must have been a dream," he muttered to himself. He brushed his hand over the crumpled mess of sheets; blankets and pillows surrounded him. As he shuffled the pillows back into position, he stopped. There was blood on the pillow.

"What's this?" He took a closer look. There was no one else in the room. He slept alone. His attendants were just outside the door. All he had to do was call and they'd come rushing to his aid.

Isobel, his wife was in another room, down the hall, still recovering from childbirth. Or so she claimed. Months ago. His son, Edward, now three months old, was in the royal nursery, carefully tended by a nursemaid. He would check on him later. He always did. It was part of his morning routine.

But this? He touched the disfigured contorted blob of red with a finger. "Still wet," he whispered, not wanting anyone to hear, even though there was no one close enough to hear unless he yelled.

"It must have been a dream," he repeated, a little loud in an attempt to reassure himself. It didn't work. The experience had been all too real. The blood was real.

He swung his legs over the side of the bed and rubbed his eyes. They felt raw, as if something had been shining brightly into his pupils for long periods of time. He ran one hand through his hair and down the back of his head. It felt tender. He could feel a scab, slightly raised. It was extremely tender to touch. He brought his hand back to the front and studied his fingers, the ones touching the scar, or whatever it was. The fingers were damp with red. Blood. He was bleeding. Not significantly, but the scab was oozing. It must be recent.

He couldn't remember the injury. Too many questions. All rather unsettling.

A knock on the door disrupted his ponderings. He flipped the pillow over to hide the evidence. He didn't want questions. Not now. He didn't have any answers. Even if he did, would anyone believe him?

He stood, allowing his nightdress to fall to his ankles as he slid his feet into the slippers which always sat next to the bed. He pulled the plaid robe off the bedpost and wrapped it around him, tying it with a sash. Satisfied he was presentable, he bellowed, "Enter."

His private secretary, distant cousin and best friend, Lord

George Bothwell, entered. "Sorry to disturb you, Your Majesty." Closing the door behind him, he left the formalities in the hall. "Henry. Are you all right? You slept awfully late. You're such an early riser. I had to make sure."

Henry waved his concerns away. George had a knack of babbling and Henry wasn't up to idle conversation. "What's the time?" he asked.

"Almost noon." George stepped further into the room. "Her Majesty has been asking after you too. You usually visit her after your breakfast. She was worried when you didn't come and she sent for me."

"She was worried, was she?" Henry didn't sound convinced.

"She said so, sir," George sidestepped the question. He understood his king's marital situation better than anyone else. On the surface and in public, all appeared to be as it should: a happily married couple enjoying the birth of their first child. A son. An heir to the Scottish throne. But deep down, there were cracks in the armor of appearances. Cracks ran deep and, as George witnessed, were exceedingly painful. The marriage was nothing more than a political farce. A sham. Instituted as an alliance between England and Scotland. Mostly to the benefit of England. George wasn't even sure if the little prince was Henry's son. But he didn't want to cause further pain to his dear friend. The man suffered enough.

Henry ran a hand through his thinning hair, grimacing as he felt again the tender spot at the back of his head. *It couldn't have been a dream. Then what happened? And why had he slept so late? George was right. Henry was always a morning person.*

"I must remind you, Cousin," George continued conversing. "The English queen arrives this afternoon. It's her annual visit and you've agreed to allow her a few weeks at your grand castle retreat."

"Balmoral." Henry sighed deeply. He had purchased the

50,000 acres on a whim over thirty years ago, built a marvelous castle and used it for his occasional retreats from the pressures of court life. Only after Queen Victoria's first visit to the nearly completed estate in 1860, she had fallen in love with the place and she been rather vocal in requesting frequent visiting rights. Her husband, Prince Albert, had been a useful aid in the castle's construction and the layout of the grounds. He and Henry had become great friends as they worked and planned together. It was considerably sad the queen's consort had died so young, only forty-two, and before the great Balmoral Estate had been completed. Their plans, Henry's and Albert's, were a big undertaking.

He shook his head to clear the cobwebs of memories. "Right," he said, more to convince himself than anyone else. "I shall get dressed and be ready for her arrival. Have some toast and tea sent up, will you George?"

"Right away." He paused briefly. "You do recall your agenda with the Arts Council. You were supposed to meet with them this afternoon, right after lunch, to finalize plans for next month's Edinburgh Arts Festival."

Henry slapped his head with the palm of his hand. "Right. Make sure the notes from the last meeting are handy so I can peruse them quickly before they arrive. Anything else?" Henry liked to be prepared. He was a vital player in his country's affairs, but he took a special interest in the arts. He fostered and nurtured what his ancestors started, creating a country internationally acclaimed as a vibrant arts centre. Scotland had reached such prestige in supporting the arts and promoting artistic endeavors in all the arts. Centuries earlier, they had become the world capital of the arts, rivalled only by Paris and Rome. Composers, painters, sculptors, dancers, actors, writers from all over the globe sought a place in Edinburgh's art world. This

Edinburgh Festival of the Arts was the place to be seen and recognized in the world of art.

"The science council will be here later this afternoon to discuss their new research project." George was rhyming off responsibilities as if he had a list in front of him. He didn't. He had a mind like a locked safe and was good at keeping Henry on track with all his commitments. "Shall I reschedule them for next week?"

"No. I'll meet with both groups. It's important I keep abreast on their activities. But thank you for the thought." Henry had moved over to the window to look out into the courtyard as George went through the list. "I do need time to settle the English royals into Balmoral and return here for some peace and quiet."

George stifled a chuckled. "Yes, sir." He cleared his throat when Henry glanced his way, with an eyebrow cocked. "Right. And Ian's here, sir. Wants an audience as soon as possible. Something about disturbances in the Highlands."

Ian MacGregor was another long-time friend and confidante. He was the Chief of the MacGregor clan, as well as a great warlord who oversaw all of Scotland's military affairs. He was a good warlord: fair and efficient. If he demanded an audience immediately, it was with good reason.

Henry wondered if Elizabeth had come with him. She was Ian's younger sister. A childhood sweetheart. Without the obligation of an English connection through marrying Isobel, Henry would have happily settled down with Elizabeth to rule the country and raise a family. Sadly, it didn't happen.

"She's not with him, sir," George spoke softly, sensing his cousin's thoughts. He cleared his throat again. "Will there be anything else?"

"Toast, George. Tea and toast. And send in Thomas." Henry's valet was as important to him as George, but in a different way. Thomas took care of Henry's personal needs. George took care of his official needs.

"Nothing else, George." Henry shook his head and waved George away. The door closed quietly behind his cousin, but the king didn't make a move to prepare himself for the day. Instead, he returned his attention to the world outside his window, allowing the sun to warm his face. He didn't see anything. He wasn't looking with intensity. He was merely staring into space. Thinking.

FOUR

Another knock on the door brought him back to his sense. "Enter." He moved from the window and stood with a hand gently placed on the back of a chair, ready to greet his valet.

Thomas entered with his usual bright, "Good morning," juggling a tray of toast and tea as he manipulated the door open, only to close it again behind him. "As requested, sir. I shall place it on the table next to your chair. Shall I move it closer to the window?" Henry answered with a brief shake of his head and Thomas continued with his chatter.

"While you have some refreshment, I shall lay out your clothes." Thomas placed the tray on the table. Henry, with a sigh of resignation, sat in the chair next to the table, watching the valet as he poured some tea and milk, not cream and sugar, as he did every morning, preparing the king's breakfast drink just the way he liked it.

"Thank you, Thomas." He forced a smile as he accepted the teacup and saucer. He could do it himself. He was not incapable of pouring tea and adding some milk and sugar. It was a simple enough task. But a valet had a job to do and he didn't want to insult his good valet by insisting he could take care of himself. It just wouldn't do. Thomas prided himself in a job well done. As did all of Henry's staff.

The valet nodded in acknowledgement as he started preparing Henry's wardrobe for the day. "It's going to be a fine day, Your Majesty," he continued with his steady stream of commentary. He was a chatty valet, but never loud or obnoxious. He just liked to talk and, he always did so in his quietly soothing voice. He neither pried nor shared gossip. Only idle chitchat. "A fine day for Queen Victoria's arrival. I gather there's already quite a crowd lining the Royal Mile, sir." He was, of course, referring to the long stretch from the grand old castle on the hill, Edinburgh Castle, to the gates of Holyrood House, including Castlehill, the Lawnmarket, the High Street, the Canongate and Abbey Strand – exactly a mile long. It was the route made famous by Queen Mary Elizabeth's first royal procession in 1603 and her ultimate proclamation in the grand courtyard of the castle. Queen Victoria's royal procession wouldn't encompass the entire route, detouring partially along Princess Street to make a more direct progression from Waverly Station where the royal train from London always made its final stop. Henry could envision it in his mind's eye. *Yes, it would be a grand procession.* His English cousin loved her pomp and circumstance parades.

He only half listened as the valet chatted on. "They like to see the English queen in all her finery, even if it is mostly black. She has the air of regal elegance and importance." The man stuttered and quickly clarified. "Oh, I not be saying you don't as well, sir. But there is a way she sits in her carriage, holding her cane with one hand and nodding her head ever so slightly in acknowledgement of those who greet her along the way."

Queen Victoria had never fully recovered from her husband's death. Even now, over twenty years later, she mourned his passing and wore the black garments of a grieving widow. She had loved Albert with such intensity. Without him, she seemed to flounder about like a ghost, oblivious to the woes of her people, taking advice from her ministers on what she should do, what foreign lands she should conquer or what foreign wars she should fight. All this while her people starved in the streets.

Henry was saddened by his cousin's lack of interest in the country's well being, relieved, too, she had no control over his Scotland. He watched his southern neighbors with interest, studying their strengths and weaknesses, but always aware the English people as a whole were mere pawns on a chessboard of life. He was a voracious reader, enjoying particularly the works of the English writer, Charles Dickens. He usually preferred Scottish authors like Walter Scott, but Dickens had a way with words and he didn't mince words as he described the drastic demise of the working class in England.

Henry banished the sad thoughts from his mind and finished his breakfast. He wasn't one for a big meal at the beginning of the day. Not like the English who enjoyed a feast to break the overnight fast. He liked to give his stomach time to wake up slowly, just as he had done this morning.

After drinking the last sip of tea, he placed the cup on its saucer and returned it to the tray. Standing up, he walked to the window to study the scene being played out below him. Indeed, the crowds were already lining the streets. Everyone was dressed in their finest to greet the English queen. They always did put on a show for visiting royals from around the world. Only a few weeks ago, the Scottish court had hosted the Russian royals, Tsar Alexander III and his family. The English had not been too happy. Queen Victoria's representative in Edinburgh had been quite vocal. The Crimean War had ended close to twenty years ago, but tensions still ran high.

Edinburgh was at its zenith of prosperity and influence and

it required a certain amount of diplomatic relations with every-one. Henry was not about to shirk his duty just because the English queen thought it was a bad idea.

"Here we are, sir." Henry stepped back from the window to see his valet laying out the wardrobe for the day. "If you care to sit, sir, I'll have your face washed and shaved in no time at all."

Thomas whipped a white sheet in the air away from his charge as Henry took his seat on the chair they saved for this purpose. It was a sleek walnut chair with horsehair-stuffed leather-covered cushions. Thomas had to spin it around in order to raise it or lower it and the back did recline to facilitate the barbering task of shaving a man's face. It was a sturdy chair, not overly comfortable, but certainly practical. Thomas kept it hidden in the corner when not in use and dragged it out daily to take care of his king's hair.

Henry settled in, resting his feet on the horsehair-stuffed leather-covered footrest and waited while Thomas placed the sheet around Henry's shoulders, tucking it in at the back. He then picked up the small jar and brush and applied well lath-ered shaving soap all over the king's face. As the valet ran the razor over the leather strap to sharpen it, Henry was lulled into a sense of compliance, soothed by the routine, but also unsettled by it. The razor met his face and the work began, stroke by stroke. Thomas was gentle. He was always gentle.

Stroke.

Wipe the razor on the towel slung over his shoulder.

Stroke.

Wipe the razor again.

It was repetitive. Gentle. Soothing.

The king hardly noticed his valet's idle chatter. When the man had put away the shaving instruments and started brushing Henry's hair, he gave a little jump when the brush met a tender spot. By the time Thomas had surveyed the cause of

Henry's discomfort, the king was fully aware of the conversation.

"You have a big cut on your head," Thomas noted as he carefully fingered the hair away from the sore spot. "Did you have a fall? It looks recent."

"No. I don't think so." Henry automatically reached up to touch the top of his head, feeling for the tender spot he had discovered earlier. What was it? Why was it there? How had it happened? Did it have something to do with his dream? Something about an implant?

Thomas put down the brush and grabbed a couple of mirrors. "Here," he said, handing the king one mirror and positioning the other mirrors so they could reflect off each other as it picked up the image of the injury. "You have a bit of a bald spot, which was concealed by your long hair hanging over it. The area looks a little raw and it appears to have stitches."

Henry studied the reflection in the mirror. He didn't remember having stitches woven into his scalp and he certainly didn't remember having a bald spot on his head. He gingerly ran his hand over the area, wincing when his coronation ring rubbed against the incision. He always referred to the ring as his coronation ring even though the only connection he knew about this ring was from his great ancestor, Queen Mary Elizabeth, who had worn it. She had passed it on to him. According to her, it had something to do with his trips through time. It did rather look like a coronation ring, though, since it bore the Royal Stuart crest. He handed the mirror back to his valet.

"I'll ask my wife," he said, trying to brush off the valet's concern. He was more disturbed than he cared to let on. "Perhaps she'll remember. Carry on, Thomas. We shall keep this between ourselves, shall we?" On second thought, he realized his wife wouldn't remember anything. She seldom took notice of him except at formal occasions. It was highly unlikely she would realize he had undergone minor surgery involving stitches. However, it might be good to make the suggestion. He had to keep up with appearances. He didn't want the downstairs staff to acknowledge what he already knew: his marriage was failing. No, he wouldn't mention it to his wife. No point.

Thomas retrieved the brush and finished brushing the king's hair, using extra care around the bald spot. Task completed. He removed the sheet from around Henry's shoulders, tossed it aside to be taken away by the cleaning staff, and proceeded towards the clothes he had laid out earlier.

"It's all right, Thomas." Henry stopped him and nodded towards the door. "I can dress myself."

"Very good, Your Majesty." Thomas sniffed, a little miffed at being dismissed. He took great pride in his job. "Will there be anything else?" Henry shook his head. Thomas let out a deep sigh to demonstrate his feelings of being slighted, as if he wasn't doing his job. He started to clear away the grooming instruments, but Henry waved him away.

"Later." Henry almost snapped. He wanted to be alone. This constant fluttering of attention was annoying at the best of times, but right now, he needed his space. Desperately.

Thomas hesitated ever so slightly. Seeing the determined look on the king's face, he decided not to argue. "Very good, Your Majesty." He let himself out of the king's chambers, closing the door quietly behind him.

FIVE

Henry managed to dress and make himself presentable in a short span of time. The nagging worry about the scar on his head and the recurring headache threatened his composure, but he had been brought up as a royal and he knew how to keep a stiff upper lip.

A knock on the door brought his thoughts into focus. "Enter."

George opened the door and stood on the threshold. "The MacGregor is waiting in your study, Your Majesty." The highland chiefs were addressed with the word "the" before the clan name, designating their rank, so to speak. Hence George's reference to Ian MacGregor, the chief of the MacGregor clan, as "The MacGregor". George had obviously shown him to the study and left him to inform the king of his presence. He knew Henry preferred to meet his friends and colleagues in a less formal environment. The study was the refuge he sought whenever he wanted to deal with matters of the realm and whenever he just wanted to unwind.

"Thank you, George. I will come right now."

"And her Majesty is requesting your presence."

"Is she now?" He quirked an eyebrow. "Well. She'll have to wait. I have business to attend to. Does she know her English cousins are arriving later this afternoon?"

Isabel was a distant cousin of Queen Victoria's. She had grown up in the English royal court alongside of the large family of princes and princesses. Being married to a king north of Hadrian's Wall had not been her choice, but Queen Victoria ruled all of her court with an iron fist and she strove to make sure all royal matches were to her benefit. A match between a young cousin, one she had raised as her own, to the neighboring monarch, was just good politics. In other words, Henry's wife was Victoria's spy in the Scottish court. Hence, Henry kept his distance and allowed Isabel little access to the political goings-on of the Scottish royal court. Unfortunately, Isabel had her own network of spies and little passed without her notice and consequently the English queen.

This current summons demanding he attend her 'court', such as it was, demonstrated yet another irksome trademark of the complex world of spies and espionage which he had to tread through. He didn't like it one bit, but he knew it was important to play the game and act the part. Little did the Scottish queen know, or the English court for that matter, Henry had his own resources and means to stay informed at all times. Not the least of these resources was his ability to jump through time and spy on those who sought to threaten his reign. Bertie, the Prince of Wales, knew of his gift, though there were times when Henry wondered if Bertie believed in time traveling, or if he thought it was just another magical trick, a slight of hand, so to speak.

As for spies in his court, he knew most of them. Some he wasn't too sure about, including George. He never let on he suspected his childhood friend. Keep your friends close and your enemies even closer, was the sage advice of the sixth century Chinese general, writer and philosopher, Sun Tzu. He held those sage words close to his heart at all times. It was good military strategy and just good sense.

"Yes," George nodded. "I believe it is why her Majesty, your wife wishes to see you. Something important she needs to discuss with you regarding their visit."

Henry groaned. "Very well. I shall pop into her chambers on my way to see Ian. Let the MacGregor know I am on the way. Make sure he has all he needs."

"Yes, Your Majesty. Already done. And I will let him know you have been slightly delayed." He bit back a knowing smile.

Henry chuckled softly. "It's all right, George. I know you understand my marital situation all too well."

"Yes, Your Majesty."

Henry made his way to his wife's chambers. He knocked, out of respect only. As king, he had every right to just march right in. In the case of his wife, he chose to give her the satisfaction of thinking she had him at her beck and call. Which in many ways she did, but only superficially.

"Enter," she called from the other side of the door.

Henry opened the door and walked in. "You requested my presence, my dear?" His voice was stiff and formal. It didn't go unnoticed.

"Yes. We must discuss our son and his need to be promised to the English." She motioned to a chair opposite her. "Sit." She spoke with the authority she falsely believed she had over him. Henry refused to oblige.

"I prefer to stand. I have meetings to attend to and you already know my position about the young prince. He will be educated in Scotland, raised as a Scottish prince and prepared to be king of Scotland. With any luck, he will find himself a fine Scottish lass to share his throne."

"No!" Isabel spat with venom. "My son will not be attached

to some poor, Scottish lass. He is meant for grander things than this backwater country."

Henry could take no more. "You have gone too far, my queen. You seem to forget yourself. You are only my wife and the mother of Scotland's prince. The title queen is merely a title and it means nothing. You would do well to remember it."

Not waiting for a response, he pivoted on his heal and stormed out of the room, making sure to pull the doors sharply shut behind him.

A few minutes later, entering the study, Ian cast a look of concern, standing to give the king due honor. "Is everything all right?" he asked his king and friend. "I heard a crash as if the walls were crumbling around us."

"Not quite." Henry marched briskly over to the table which held his prized whisky and glasses. He lifted the lid off the bottle and held it up as he glanced at Ian. "Shall I pour you a glass? I think I could drink the entire bottle right now."

Ian chuckled. "Must be wife problems. I shall join you, my friend. And I shall make sure you do not have too much. We wouldn't want you tipsy with the English monarch almost on your doorstep, now would we?"

"I don't see why not!" The king smirked at his friend as he poured two glasses. Carrying them across the room, he handed one to Ian. They raised their glasses and clinked them together. "To the women in our lives. May they be forever meek, humble and somewhere else."

Ian laughed and the men tossed the contents, glass full, down their throats. "Ahh! Better." Henry wasn't usually a drinking man, but sometimes the stress was too much to bear. Like this morning, with his bad dreams, sore scab on his head (throbbing head, too) and a nagging wife who believed she ran the show always lording it over him whenever she could.

"Another?" he asked Ian, who shook his head, placing the glass on a nearby table.

"No. I'm fine. Thanks. Can't handle the drink as I once could."

Placing his glass on the table as well, Henry reconciled himself to the need to remain sober. At least for now. "I know what you mean. Now what brings you to Edinburgh? I know how much you dislike the big city, so it must be serious." He waved for Ian to be seated and lowered himself into a chair.

"It is." Ian leaned forward in his chair and rubbed his hands together. "I fear the English have infiltrated our land, Your Majesty. And they're raising havoc amongst our highland chiefs, causing mischief and making every clan fear the other clan has joined ranks with the English."

Henry rubbed his forehead. He needed another glass of whisky. He didn't need another problem. Especially with the English queen almost on his doorstep. "How did this start, Ian? And what proof do you have?"

Ian stood up and made his way to the reading table beneath a long row of bookshelves. Henry followed him, concern evident as he took great care in this room to make sure everything was where he could find it. The table, often covered with books and maps, was the one Henry used frequently when studying documents, reading up on historical details, and laying out plans. It was usually a mess. One end had been carefully cleared, the books and documents neatly organized at the opposite end. At least, he hoped they were organized. He had been deep into his plans for the expansion of Scotland's National Gallery of Art when fatigue drove him to bed the previous night. He restrained his concern, focusing on the item displayed across the cleared portion of the table.

"This," Ian unbound the cloth to reveal the long sword. "The hilt gave it away. It's an English sword." Ian stated the obvious.

The guard had an intricate design, woven in metal, depicting the statant guardant lion in the center, wearing the St. Edward's Crown, the crown jewel of England, named after Edward the Confessor. It was supported by a similarly crowned English lion. The Tudor rose was evident in the foliage at the base of the guard beneath the lions and all was surrounded by the Garter circlet. On the pommel, in fine letters, was the Latin phrase, the English chivalrous Order of the Garter's motto, *Honi soit qui mal y pense*".

"Shame on him who thinks evil," Henry spoke softly, translating the Latin words into English. "Definitely English. Where did you find this?"

Ian held up his hand to ward off further questions. "Wait. I will explain. But there is more." He removed the cloth on another item. At first glance it had the appearance of a sheath for a smaller sword or even a knife. Ian slid his finger into the opening at one end and carefully slipped out a piece of paper. He unrolled it on the desk and motioned for Henry to look closely.

"It's in code," Henry studied it closely. "I think I recognize the code. Bertie, I mean the Prince of Wales, and I developed this code as children. We used to have great fun sending secret messages to each other." He studied the message, muttering under his breath as he tried to unravel its secrets. "I think I have it. It reads: The prince is the key. Watch. Wait. When family goes to Balmoral," he pointed at an abstract symbol, a box, with two towers, one on either end. "Look, our own secret sign for the castle." He continued to read his translation. "Take the infant, Prince Edward, Crown Prince of Scotland, and his mother." He stepped back, a look of fear, mixed with shock and anger marking his facial expression. "They plan to kidnap my son. And he's using my code, our secret code, to pass on the message.

To whom? And did he not think I might see the message and be able to decipher it?"

"We can't let it happen," Ian rolled the parchment and returned it to the sheath for safekeeping. "Lock up these things." He gave the king a stern look of warning. "You may need them later."

Henry nodded. Before he could remove the evidence of England's betrayal, the doors burst open behind them and the Prince of Wales pranced in.

"Bertie!" Henry exclaimed as he marched to greet his cousin, masking his concern about the prince arriving at the moment when Henry was learning of yet another ploy by the English against the Scots. In spite of his unease at being caught unravelling an English plot, Henry cared for his cousin and he couldn't help but notice Bertie's appearance. The Prince of Wales had aged considerably since Henry had last seen him. *Too much booze and women,* he supposed. He was only about ten years older than Henry, but he appeared to be twice his age.

Henry and Bertie weren't first cousins by any means, but as with all royal houses, there was a direct line of ancestry which conveniently connected one royal to another. Henry was a Stuart, a direct descendant of Mary Queen of Scots through her daughter, Queen Mary Elizabeth, who took the throne of Scotland after her brother, James, chose the English crown over the Scottish one. King James VI of Scotland became King James I of England, originally planning to amalgamate Scotland to England. The Scottish people would have none of it, the depth of animosity between the two peoples going too deep and too far back in time. The newly recognized Princess Mary Elizabeth claimed the Scottish throne and it was her ancestors who continued to rule Scotland and make it a strong nation, independent and free. Henry continued the progress his great ancestor started.

Queen Victoria, a distant descendant of King James I, continued to barter with her northern neighbors in the hopes to complete the amalgamation her ancestor failed to do. She attempted controlling Henry, even though the marriage to Isabel had failed. Henry cared for his English cousins, but he was determined to keep the border between the two countries strong and well fortified. His people were Scottish, not some amalgamated conglomerate under the iron rule of the English. He was determined to keep it this way.

He enjoyed the family connection. How could he not? He was an only child and the appearance of the English royal family in the Scottish court at least once a year was a grand event. He and Bertie were more than just cousins. They were friends. Good friends. During those summers of his youth, growing up, getting into mischief together, Henry had idolized Bertie. And the others, too: Alfred, Arthur, and Leopold. He had been closer in age to Arthur, but all the young princes idolized the Prince of Wales, Albert Edward, whom everyone within the royal circle called Bertie.

The princes had bonded well. But not the girls. They had always been too prissy for Henry's liking. Though he suspected the queen hoped for a match between him and one of her brood. "We must join the two countries," she frequently said. The closest to joining he could abide was marrying Isabel. And, it was a rash act of madness, if he had to be honest with himself. Every time Victoria visited, which she always did on her way to Balmoral, she only had time for Isabel. According to his ears within his court, all the two did was plot. Henry was determined to prevent the amalgamation of Scotland and England. Victoria was determined to make sure the two countries did blend and co-exist as one.

"Finally. I am here at last." The Prince of Wales always loved a bit of drama. It was not unusual for him to storm into a room unannounced and catch the people within unawares. "You have no idea how difficult it is to spend an entire day with my mother." After sharing a jubilant embrace with his cousin, the prince noticed Ian standing by the table, trying to quickly wrap the evidence he had been showing Henry only minutes before. Walking around Henry, Bertie made his way to the table, ignoring Ian's tip of head, acknowledging his rank and privilege. "What have we here?" He stopped and his face paled with concern and then changed abruptly to beat red with anger. "What's this? You have one of my men's swords!"

"So, you admit it's yours?" It was as much a statement as a question, but Henry was studying his cousin closely while at the same time trying to guard his tongue.

"Of course, it's one of mine. Now the question is, what are you two doing with it?" he snapped.

Henry nodded to Ian, allowing him to explain. "It was taken from a dead soldier, your highness. A dead English soldier. One of many who have been invading our highlands and causing mischief amongst our people."

"Impossible!" the prince sputtered. "Why would one of my men be fighting in the highlands?"

"We have a right to know, Bertie." Henry crossed his arms in front of his chest and all but glared at his cousin with determined fierceness. "Would you care to enlighten us, Cousin?"

"There must be a mistake." The man was a bundle of nervous energy. "Someone is trying to set me up and make me look bad. I am convinced of it."

"And using our own secret code to give orders?" Henry couldn't resist.

"Secret code?" Bertie started fidgeting, his hands wringing each other with ferocity as he shuffled from one foot to the other. "What do you mean, secret code?"

"The one we devised and used as children, Bertie," Henry

insisted. *Bertie was guilty of something. It was obvious. But what?* It remained to be determined. He removed the coded message from its protective sheath and, unraveling it, handed it to Bertie. "It's giving orders to kidnap my son, Bertie. Why?"

The prince visibly blanched, his guilt written all over his face. He stuttered as sweat built up on his brow and started trickling down his cheeks. He pulled out a handkerchief and wiped it viciously away. He was about to crumble the paper, but Henry was too quick. He snatched it out of Bertie's hand before damage could be done to the evidence.

"I don't know what to say, Henry." Bertie cleared his throat and coughed into the handkerchief he continued to hold. "Mother made me do it." His eyes darted around the room, refusing to latch onto Henry's.

"Hmm!" Henry exclaimed. "Quite possible. She still has you under her thumb, doesn't she?" Bertie squirmed at the accusation. He was sensitive to the fact he was only the Prince of Wales with no rights or privileges or power, other than his royal title. Henry handed the message to Ian who efficiently returned it to the sheath.

The following silence was eerie.

Unsettling.

Henry watched. And waited.

Bertie broke the silence with another nervous cough. "Yes. Well. It's how it is, my friend."

"Friend?" Henry snorted. "Is this how you treat your friends? By kidnapping their children?"

"My mother..."

"Yes, I know." Henry waved his hand as if to silence the man and his excuses. "We all know about your mother."

"She is probably in your wife's chambers now, plotting her next move."

It may have been a ploy to remove Henry from the study. Or

it may have been an attempt to make amends. Henry glanced at Ian. "Stay here, Ian. Guard the evidence."

Ian nodded and Henry made a quick exit, heading for his wife's rooms. He made it to the main hall, just as the black-clad queen from south of the border made her entrance. Henry took several deep breaths, straightened his shoulders and posed as the welcoming royal host. He walked forward to greet her with outstretched hands. She stopped halfway across the room and stomped her cane with decided force. "Where is she?" Her eyes glazed Henry's. "Where is your wife? She couldn't be bothered to come greet her cousin?"

Henry was obviously inconsequential. He bowed his head solicitously, greeting in a barely civil voice, "Greetings, Cousin."

The queen flashed him an icy glare. "Well?" She stomped her cane again.

"Still resting, Your Majesty." Although a king of equal rank as his southern neighbor, Henry greeted Victoria with the formal recognition of her position.

She responded in kind, though not as warm as one would expect from a visiting monarch. "Your Majesty. My cousin gave birth over a month ago. I birthed many children and was always up and about within a day or two. No excuse for this. Take me to her." Noticing the hesitance, she punctuated her demand. "Now!"

"Yes, Ma'am." Henry bowed slightly and started to lead the way.

"No, not you, Henry." She let out a deep sigh signifying her frustration. "Must I explain everything. Bertie." She waved her hand dismissively. "Go play with my boy. This man will escort me." She pointed her cane at George who was hovering in the shadows.

"Yes, Cousin." He nodded to George to carry on, fully

intent on following close behind. At least, after he finished interrogating Bertie.

Henry watched the retreating figure of the English queen as she sashayed down the hall, her long black gown trailing behind her like a wisp of foreboding. He shook his head. First his wife's attempt at making demands for their son; then Ian's revelation the English were causing mischief in the highlands and threatening to kidnap his son. *Oh yes, and the dream which wasn't a dream. Or was it?* There was the scar and its unknown origins. Something about an implant. He shook his head to try and clear his thoughts and instantly regretted the sudden movement as the room started to spin.

"Are you all right, Your Majesty?" One of the guards stationed by the main door appeared before Henry.

The room settled to a normal keel as Henry acknowledged his reassurances with a warm smile. "Thank you, young man. You are observant. I am fine, now. Just fine." He marched off to rejoin Bertie in the study. He had questions to ask his cousin. Lots of questions.

He walked into the study, closing the door quietly behind him. Bertie was sitting facing the hearth, an empty glass in one hand and a freshly lit cigar in the other. He had found Henry's stash of goodies and helped himself. Both Ian and the evidence were gone.

Bertie perked up when he heard the door open. "He just left. Took the evidence with him." The prince placed the cigar between his lips and took another deep puff, before taking it out and placing it in the ashtray on the table next to him. He set down the empty glass and rose to greet his cousin. "I am sorry, Cousin. I had no idea."

Henry studied Bertie. The man seemed sincere enough. But was he? Someone had shared their secret code. It had to be Bertie because it certainly wasn't Henry. After a lengthy silence, he nodded, deciding to accept his cousin at his word. For now. He would keep him under close surveillance though. Both Bertie and his mother. Not to mention Henry's own wife and her lackey of devoted followers.

The two men embraced fondly, patting each other on the back. Henry pulled away first, choosing a topic other than spies and plots. "Sorry to hear about Leopold's illness. I had hoped he would join you this time." The youngest English prince had always been sickly, but his illnesses were complicated by an inherited disease. Hemophilia. A curse of royalty. Too much inbreeding, Henry believed, but no one accepted his theory. "We write, you know. Good lad. Smart. Very much like his father, don't you think?"

"Yes. He is smart, isn't he?" Bertie was rather ruffled at the reference to his younger brother. He was never comfortable with others receiving the praise he felt he deserved.

"Anyone else come with you?" Henry asked.

"Later," was the curt answer. "They'll join as at Balmoral."

"Splendid."

Bertie retrieved his cigar and held it up in acknowledgement. "Fine cigar, Henry. Very fine indeed."

"It's my latest shipment of those Jamaican cigars you enjoyed the last time you were here." Scotland had long been a powerful force on the oceans, colonizing islands and continents around the world. England and Scotland each had their domains, a rivalry which didn't go unnoticed. Scotland had long since colonized Jamaica, encouraging the agricultural potentials of the island, particularly its ability to easily grow tobacco. They developed a fine cigar, one rivalling the Cuban cigar. Cuba, after all, was an English colony.

"Splendid!" Bertie beamed, placing it between his lips again and closing his eyes as he enjoyed the experience. The men took seats facing each other. "Where's Uncle Harry?" Bertie asked. "I haven't seen him in quite some time."

Uncle Harry was the name used to address the king when he jumped through time and visited himself and his family in the past. Like his ancestor a few centuries earlier, Queen Mary Elizabeth, King Henry's memories of his first adventure traveling through time was unnerving. He had been shocked and, as a young lad at the time, hadn't fully comprehended what was happening and why.

The king hesitated ever so slightly before answering. It was not a question he expected to hear. Not from his cousin. Bertie was many things, but he seldom remembered people, especially those he saw so infrequently. He pulled himself together, shifting his gaze restlessly. Taking a deep breath, silent, contained, he forced a smile.

"He travels a lot." Henry sat back in his chair and crossed one leg over the other to portray a posture of relaxation. "He was just here last month, Bertie. You missed him. Next time I see him, I'll be sure to mention you were asking after him."

"You do that." Bertie allowed the cigar to dangle between his lips as he talked. He stretched out his legs and leaned his head back to study his cousin closely. "You know, Henry. Funny thing is. I've studied our family trees. And I can't find any trace of your Uncle Harry."

The king froze. Briefly. Every so slightly. He quickly composed himself. "Really? It's strange."

"How is it he's related?" The prince removed the cigar and knocked it in the tray, as he waited Henry's response.

"I never said he was related." Henry took his time to explain. "He's an uncle by name, only because he's always been such a close family friend. No blood relation."

"Ah! But it doesn't explain why he looks so much like you

and his mannerisms are so similar. Are you sure you're not related?"

Henry all but beamed. "Quite sure."

A knock on the door interrupted their conversation. "Enter." Henry gave the command.

George poked his head inside. "I have seen Her Majesty the English queen to Her Majesty's private chambers, Your Majesty."

"Too many majesties," Bertie grumbled through the cigar once again perched between his lips.

Henry coughed to stifle a chuckle. "Very good, George. Would you care to join us?"

George stepped into the room. "No thank you, Your Majesty. But I did find someone just coming in from the court-yard. Someone you might like to see."

An older man stepped in behind George and made his way directly to the young king. With a nod, George slipped out, closing the door behind him. "Uncle Harry." Henry jumped to his feet to greet his guest. The two Henry's hugged fondly, slapping each other on the back. Stepping back young Henry observed his older self. At least thirty years older, judging by the fading hairline and the greying around the temples. The older Henry, Uncle Harry, must have noted the entry in the journal which suggested he visit on this day, to quell any further questions from their cousin, Bertie. "We were just talking about you. Bertie claims he hasn't seen you in years."

Uncle Harry laughed. "Well, now. What a coincidence. And here I am." He marched over to where Bertie still sat and extended his hand in greeting. He bobbed his head and gave the perfunctory greeting expected for royalty, "Your highness."

"Yes, isn't it so," Bertie stuck the cigar in his mouth and left it there while he grasped the older man's hand. "So where have you been?"

"Here and there. And everywhere in between." Uncle Harry was good at vague responses. This was about as vague as one could get. "I tried popping in to see you last time I was in London. Only I discovered you were at someone's private castle or lodge or something of the sort. Can't keep track of you, my boy. Can't keep track of you. I do believe we have all aged somewhat since we last met." He ran a hand through what hair remained on his scalp. Bertie just grunted in response. "And, I hear you are happily married with children of your own. Three boys and three girls."

"Only two boys, now. Young Alex died shortly after he was born."

"Ah yes! I remember now. Very sad."

Bertie merely shrugged. If he still felt the pain of loss, he didn't show it.

"And they'll all be married off soon, no doubt." Uncle Harry carried on the friendly banter, trying to put Bertie at ease. Not a simple task at the best of times. "I hear there's plans to match one of your girls with Henry's newborn."

"Pshaw!" Bertie snorted and took a deep inhale of his cigar. "Young Prince Edward, Crown Prince of Scotland, is only a few month's old. Too young for any of my daughters. Even my youngest, Maud, at six, is a little old for the young prince. And they're both too young to plan a wedding. No." He shook his head vehemently, eyes darting about nervously. "It won't happen."

The young king had moved to the side table and poured three glasses of whisky. He handed one to Bertie and another to Uncle Harry before lifting it in a salute, clinking his glass with the others in turn. "Ah. Thank you, lad." The older Henry took a sip. "Fine stuff. A cigar for your old uncle?" He reached into the offered box, choosing the one closest. He ran it under his nose. Satisfied, he bit off the tip, disposing it and placed the cigar between his lips. The king lit a match and helped him light up. Inhaling, the older man pondered only slightly his next words. "Well, now. Being a royal means you're a pawn on the chessboard. Age doesn't matter. Something your mother knows extremely well. I have it on good authority she's upstairs with the Queen of Scotland right now plotting and planning for Maud and Edward to become a couple."

"No!" Bertie slapped his glass down. "I won't have it. I tell you, I won't."

"Well, if not Maud, then who?"

Bertie snapped, almost spitting out his cigar. "What's with the woman anyway? Always plotting and planning everyone's lives to suit herself." He shook his head. "Henry." He stood up, giving his cousin a steely gaze. "We have to stop this now. Are you with me?"

"Absolutely," the king downed the rest of his whisky and stood up to accompany his cousin. It was time to confront the Queen of England and set things straight. What better ally than the Prince of Wales. "Uncle Harry." He patted the older man's shoulder affectionately. "Until next time."

Sensing his presence was no longer required or desired, he responded in kind, "Until next time."

SIX

Bertie was two steps behind Henry as he stormed out of the study, stomping his way along the halls and up the grand staircase to the second level. As they approached Isabel's chambers, Henry steamed at the gull of both his wife and the English queen. He was forever pondering the politics and, yes, the benefits of royal marriages. The last thing he wanted to do was dictate who should marry whom, especially where his child was concerned. He wanted him to be allowed the choice. *Within reason*, he supposed. Ideally, a marriage between his son and the daughter of one of his loyal dukes would be the best option. All he could do was introduce possible choices and allow his son to make the final selection.

If only he had chosen more wisely. He realized now, too late, he hadn't made a good choice in a marriage partner. If he could go back, he would have chosen someone else, a childhood sweetheart. However, he had believed he loved Isabel, or at least he could love her if he tried. He believed she loved him in return, enough to make it work between them. All too soon after their marriage, Henry learned it was pomp and circumstance for Isabel: the glittery jewels, flashy gowns and the obeisance of an entire kingdom. What more could a girl ask for? He had hoped for more. His great ancestor, Queen Mary Elizabeth, hadn't been able to marry her love choice, but she hadn't done too bad in her marriage partner. They had been friends and partners throughout their married life. Which accounted for more than most royal marriages.

But Henry and Isabel? Friends? Not even close?

"Henry?" Bertie had stopped abruptly and was scowling at his cousin. "Henry?"

"Hmm!" The king was startled from his thoughts. They had reached his wife's door. "Hmm!" He muttered again. "Yes, I agree. Not a good idea. Maud is much too old for my son." He paused briefly and without sharing a glance at his cousin stated quite firmly, "Just like your mother though, to try yet again to amalgamate our two countries. Will the royals of England never learn?" He was re-stating the arguments they had already shared back in the study. "What your mother can't seem to understand, and I hope you do, is Scotland doesn't want to become part of England."

Bertie showed hesitance in barging into the chambers of his host's wife, even with the wife's husband, the King of Scotland, standing next to him. Had he been on home soil, he wouldn't have thought twice about doing such a thing. Henry had no qualms however. After his brief pause and verbal outburst, he reached for the door handle. A clipped English voice caused him to hesitate and listen.

Queen Victoria was speaking. He could hear her voice through the closed door as if he were standing before her. "You must stand up to him, Isabel," she was scolding his wife. "He needs to be made to understand. Scotland and England belong together. This dream the Stuarts have carried with them for so long, since the days of Queen Mary Elizabeth. It's a dream serving no purpose, other than to bolster Scottish egos. One must move on towards progress. And Scotland would fare much better as England's ward than it has done on its own. You, Isabel, must make sure he gives you more children, more heirs to marry off to English suitors. More means to bring our two countries together."

He had heard enough. Scotland didn't need England. It was the other way around. While Scotland progressed ahead of so many other countries in literature, the arts, science and colonization, England floundered trying to keep up. Scotland was a thorn in England's side and England was not going to let the Scottish thorn go unchecked. Not for long anyway. England wanted what King James I promised and couldn't deliver. England wanted domination over the entire British Isles. Which included Scotland. It wasn't going to happen.

He didn't bother to knock. Turning the knob, he slammed the door back and barged into the room with Bertie right on his heels. "How dare you!" He pointed an accusing finger at the English queen. "You come here as my guest and turn my wife against me and my country and demand we, the rulers of Scotland and England, become one. It is something, my dear queen, which will never happen. And the sooner you realize the simple fact the better. There will not be any more heirs. Not from me. Not with this woman. I will not take this woman to my bed again. You have both deceived me and threatened my throne and my country. As of today, Queen Isabel will have no powers in this country. She will be removed to Loch Leven Castle, a fitting retreat for a captive queen, don't you think?" He almost beamed as he saw the stunned look on both queens' faces. "I will choose her companions and she will have no access to my son. Not now. Not ever. Scotland is free and independent. FOR NOW AND FOREVER!" He spat out the final words with increasing volume, the battle cry which had driven Queen Mary Elizabeth to power and secured her throne.

Turning to leave, he almost tripped over his cousin. The stunned look on Bertie's face didn't stop Henry. He was too angry. Infuriated. Glancing back at the two queens, he pointed maliciously at his wife. "Pack your things, Isabel. You leave within the hour." He didn't react when she cried out in dismay. He was on a rampage and no woman's tears could stop him. Not now. Not ever.

"And Queen Victoria," he quickly added. "You will leave immediately as well. I will have my royal guards personally escort you and your family out of my country. You are no longer welcome in Scotland. You will no longer be granted access to Balmoral." He pushed Bertie aside and stomped towards the door. He reached the threshold and paused to add one more verbal punch. "Perhaps I'll have it pulled down and the land leased out to starving northern English farmers who need good land to make a living. If they pledged allegiance to Scotland, they would be welcome here."

Bertie gasped at the list of demands and orders. "Henry." He reached out to his cousin, but Henry shook him off.

"You'll have to leave too, Bertie." Henry's voice was lower, but with all the evidence stacking up, even Bertie's words of reassurance fell on deaf ears. There was nothing Bertie or his mother could say now to change Henry's position.

Bertie's mother wasn't one to back down so easily. "You wouldn't dare!" Queen Victoria's voice almost sounded like a snarl. She could be an annoyingly dominating monarch when she set aside her grief for a husband long since dead.

Henry caught the piercing gaze and held it with one of his own, equally piercing. "I do dare, Madam!" He snapped back. "This is my realm. Not yours. And it never shall be yours!" He almost spat out the last few words. He was adamant to make his point: Scotland, his country, would remain free and independent, for now and forever, as his countryman's rallying cry firmly stated.

"Then Isabel comes home to London with me." The English queen sniffed in a deep breath, feigning a sense of pride being wounded. "It's where she belongs."

"I think not!" Henry held his ground, glancing first at his wife then at the English queen.

"Why ever not, Henry?" Bertie gently challenged Henry. "She is obviously not wanted here."

"Bertie's right, Henry." Isabel finally spoke between sniffles and catching little coughs, feigning an upset constitution. "I should return with my English cousins. London is my home. It always has been. Not this barren, cold north land."

"No!" He glared at both women, then at Bertie who had moved closer to his mother during the interchange. "The last time a Scottish queen sought refuge in England under the protection of the English queen, the Scottish queen lost her head."

"Now wait a minute here, Henry," Bertie tried to interrupt. He didn't get the chance to say anything else.

"You stay out of this." Henry pointed an accusing finger at his cousin.

"Yes, Bertie." Victoria took her son's arm and patted it gently as if soothing a distraught child. "It's best you stay out of this. You don't know what you're talking about." Bertie stiffened visibly at his mother's comment, but no one appeared to notice.

Isabel was the one who was distraught. She continued on her rampage, trying desperately to make her points clear, to avoid her banishment to the isolated castle which was reputed to be haunted by a beheaded queen who screamed around her tower prison on a nightly basis. "Instead you send me to the island castle which held another queen prisoner." They were both referring to Queen Mary I of Scotland, often referred to as the captive Queen of Scots since she spent more years of her reign in captivity than she did as a ruling monarch. Loch Leven had been her prison before she escaped to England where the English imprisoned her in various castles until at last, her cousin Queen Elizabeth I signed the decree to have Queen Mary beheaded at Fotheringay Castle. Beheaded in England, but doing her haunting in Scotland.

Henry faked a smile, his eyes focussed on Isabel. "True enough. But at least at Loch Leven you'll be allowed to keep your head." Turning back to the English queen, he added with a snarky tone of voice, "Which is more than I can assure you should you put your trust in England and the English queen."

Queen Victoria let out a disgruntled huff. Before anyone could speak further on the matter, Henry made his departure with great fanfare and drama. He marched out of his wife's chambers. He left the door ajar, calling out as he exited the chambers.

"Guards." Footsteps paraded from either direction. "Escort the English queen and her son to Waverly Station. Make sure all of the attendants and accumulated luggage is loaded securely on the train. Our guests leave at once." As the gathered guards followed their orders, Henry called for more guards and ordered them to escort his wife to Loch Leven Castle. "She may take one attendant and one change of clothes. There is little time to pack. She must be gone within the hour. And she must be kept under constant supervision and locked securely at the castle. In Queen Mary's tower."

"And the infant prince, Your Majesty?" Henry was asked by one of the guards.

"My son, Prince Edward, remains with me." Then he stomped down the hall, assured his orders would be carried out without question. He needed another drink. His head was throbbing and his anger was seething through his veins.

"How dare you!" Queen Victoria's voice followed him down the hall. Though small in stature, she had a powerful presence, which she exuded to the fullest when deemed necessary. This was one of those occasions. "I have exceptionally powerful allies, young man. You would do well to heed my advice. Alienating me will do you more harm than good."

Henry stopped at the top of the grand staircase. Without turning, he bellowed his response. "I have powerful friends and allies, too, Madam. I would advise you to be wary of my abilities to protect my lands and my people. Do not threaten me, Madam. And do not interfere with my country, my people, my politics, my wife and family ever again. Do you understand?" Henry had never been so angry. His face flushed beet red as he almost yelled at his southern neighbor.

Turning to the guards still marching up the stairs he ordered, "Don't let either queen out of your sight and keep them apart. I need a guard on my son, as well. His attendants must be watched until we can replace them with people only I can trust."

"Yes, Your Majesty."

"Henry." Isabel called from her rooms. She used the voice she saved for special occasions, like when she wanted something desperately. She knew how to put on the charm when needed. "Can we talk?"

He returned to the chambers and stood at the door, glaring at his wife. He was relieved to see the English royals had been escorted out. "Speak your mind, woman. For after this day, we shall speak to each other no more." His voice was a low growl, just loud enough to project his message. He was angry. Hurt. Annoyed. Disgusted.

"How can you do this to me? Send me away from you, from my son? How? What have I done to deserve this?" She was whining, now. She walked over to her husband, reaching to take his hands in hers. He pulled them back, stepping away.

"You are a traitor," he said, his voice cold and distant. He would honor this woman no more. She had deceived him. "You have used your manipulative charms to spy on my country, on my people, on me. You have plotted against my wishes. My son, only days after his Christening, and you are already marrying him off to some English princess. I know now I made a mistake in marrying an English princess and I will never allow the same for my son. Don't you realize?" He held an accusing finger just inches from her face, his eyes ablaze with anger. "Don't you realize the English only want to dominate us? It's all they've ever wanted."

"No, Henry." Isabel shook her head, stepping away from the finger still mocking her. "You're wrong. They want to make both our countries stronger. By working together as one, we could be a very powerful nation."

"Scotland already is a very powerful nation!" Henry was yelling. His anger was taking control, something he tried to avoid at all cost. "England wants the Scottish Empire to be theirs. England wants the Scottish lands and people to pay taxes to the English crown. England wants the Scottish people to fight their battles. No! It's why my great ancestor, Queen Mary Elizabeth, took the throne from her brother, James when he tried to amalgamate the two countries. She wanted to protect Scottish rights and freedoms forever. And I want the same. Obviously, you don't."

"I want what's best for all of us, Henry." Isabel spoke more quietly than her husband. It no longer mattered. Henry had stormed out of her room. He needed a drink.

SEVEN

Henry was about to pour a glass of whisky when there was a knock on the door and George poked his head in. Henry set the decanter down, leaving his drink for later. He didn't usually drink during the day and even less so in the morning, but these were extenuating circumstances. Besides, his head hurt like a sledgehammer was rattling around inside his skull.

Rubbing his brow as if he could erase the pain within, he let out a deep, pent-up sigh and said, "Yes, George."

"The arts council members are waiting in the receiving rooms and the science council are just arriving for their briefing. I've had them directed to the drawing room. Shall I serve refreshments and tell them you will be with them shortly?" All business. George was always good at putting on a professional, business-like air.

In all the foray and confrontations with the two queens and the Prince of Wales, Henry had forgotten George's earlier reminder. "Yes, George. That would be fine. I will meet with the arts council first. Some sandwiches and a light beverage would be nice. I feel as if I could use some fortification as well." Looking at the clock on the mantle, he was surprised to see it was after twelve. It had been a busy morning. Then again, he had arisen a little later than usual.

The Edinburgh Arts Festival. One of the highlights on his calendar. His ancestor, Queen Mary Elizabeth had initiated the project to not only nurture the growing arts community in Scotland, but also to encourage artists from around the world to at least visit if not participate. The entire Edinburgh Castle was taken over by the arts community for the month of July each year. The halls displayed countless works by rising stars in the arts community, like this new group known as the Impressionists, Claude Monet and Edgar Degas. These artists had frequently shown their works at several exhibits in Edinburgh and Glasgow over the past few years. The Scots seem to applaud what the French could not, the vision of impressions created on canvas. Henry had become close friends with several of these artists. Claude and Edgar being frequent guests at either Holyrood House or Balmoral, were starting to voice their desire to settle permanently in Scotland.

"The countryside beckons, Your Majesty," Claude said during his last visit. "The mists and the fogs help inspire our creative visions. This land is for impressionistic endeavors, don't you agree?"

Nothing further was said, but Henry expected to have dinner with Claude and others over the course of the month-long festival. He would learn more then. He hoped he could entice them to take up residence on a more permanent basis. He even had a plan in motion to construct an artist community in the heart of the highlands.

The festival featured literary works as well. There would be readings by current authors like the French Symbolist poet, Stéphane Mallarmé, and the Scottish born mystery writer, Sir Arthur Ignatius Conan Doyle. Plays and musical concerts would be featured in the grand hall and open-air events would also welcome visitors in the castle's grand courtyard. It was a big event. Even bigger than the famed Salon de Paris. The Edinburgh Arts Festival encouraged and promoted the new and the daring in all the creative arts. The Salon de Paris was only interested in academic works duplicating what had been done for centuries.

Henry straightened his jacket and fussed with his collar, rotating his head around to stretch and sooth his neck muscles. He made his way to the receiving rooms, following George and allowing him to announce his presence.

George did so in great style. He swung open the double doors and announced in a booming voice, "His Majesty, King Henry I of Scotland." Stepping back, he bowed his head, allowing Henry to walk into the room to greet a row of now standing and respectfully quiet men and women, all with their heads bowed. The solitary woman curtsied as he approached.

"Robert, Margaret, Billy." Henry walked around the room greeting everyone by name, returning to his two closest artist friends, the writers Robert Louis Stevenson and Margaret Todd. Margaret was a teacher, but Henry knew she had great potential. Having visited her in the future, he knew she would one day become a fine doctor and a novelist.

"Robert. Glad to have you back from the Riviera." He studied the man closely. "You do look better than the last time I saw you." The Scottish climate didn't always agree with the writer and Robert often took long sojourns to the sunny French Riviera to recuperate and to delve deeper into his writing muse.

"I am much improved, Your Majesty. And always pleased to return to Edinburgh in time to help with the annual festival." Robert had been instrumental in promoting the event over the past few years. Henry often wondered what he would do without him.

"Billy. I loved the painting you gifted me of Balmoral at

sunset. Absolutely splendid array of light and colors, well blended for extra effect. But you must allow me to purchase your works. You shouldn't be giving it all away." Billy, or William McTaggart, had been strongly influenced by the French Impressionists, but chose to remain in Scotland and use his talents to capture the beauty of the Scottish landscape. He also painted marine scenes and could often be found roaming the extensive coastline of Scotland, as well as its major harbours at Edinburgh and Greenock.

Billy and Henry had been close friends since the day, as children, they stumbled upon one another, quite literally, in an isolated glen in the highlands. Even as a youngster, Billy was always out in the wilds sketching. It's what he was doing when Henry and Ian were racing their mounts through the thick brush and almost trampled the young artist. A few sketches were torn up by the horses' hooves in the process, something Billy never let Henry and Ian forget, but otherwise there was no damage and a strong friendship between the men staggered out of the initial anger on Billy's part for his damaged art and Henry's part for the race he was winning before he had to pull up short.

Standing before the only woman in the group, Henry studied the woman. She was a bit young to be on a planning committee such as this. She came highly recommended, though. A teacher as well as a passionate follower of the arts, she was a good choice to keep the others on track, on schedule and organized. This was her first year with the council and Henry was quickly learning to respect her areas of expertise. "Have you given further thought to writing your novel, Margaret?" he asked. "At the last meeting, you were suggesting you might write a novel some day."

Margaret look a bit startled at her king's familiarity. She wouldn't have thought a man who met so many people each day and was responsible for the entire country would remember her after just a few committee meetings. To top it off, remember a comment she made at random about possibly taking up the art of writing. "Not yet, Your Majesty." She gave the king a demure smile. "But some day I hope to write it. Right now, my students keep me awfully busy."

"I'm sure they do." Henry nodded in agreement. "I hear you are doing a fine job, though. Reverend Scott is all praise when discussing your merits as a teacher."

Margaret blushed again. The king had been checking up on her. She didn't mind. It was understandable he would want to know a little more about her. She was young. She knew it. She had only been teaching for a couple of years. She had been hired on by Reverend Scott, one of the first teachers at the newly built Abbeyhill Primary School on Regent Road. It wasn't far from Holyrood House, but it certainly didn't mean the students came from wealthy families. On the contrary, most of the students were from working class families. Not like the working class in England who were mostly impoverished. Scotland would never allow it. All Scots were given free education and equal privileges to their peers; equal in the sense of allowing them the opportunities to succeed and prosper should their learning lead them in a certain direction. For this Margaret was thankful. Had she not been allowed an education, she would never be a teacher herself and probably married off to some working-class man with a herd of children at her feet. It was not a pleasant thought.

"Sorry we are late." The door swung open dramatically behind the gathering and everyone glanced at the intruder.

"Hamish, Hector, Gladys," Henry greeted the late arrivals. Two musicians and an actress. In London, the actress would be considered nothing more than a prostitute; in Edinburgh, it was considered an art form and revered as such. Gladys McCordick was an artist in her trade and an exceptionally fine actress. She had performed many leading female roles, like Lady Macbeth in Shakespeare's Scottish set play, *Macbeth*, as well as many other powerful roles. Hamish MacCunn and Hector MacCallum were late Romantic composers who painted in music the true spirit of the Scottish people and their land.

"Your Majesty." Hamish and Hector bowed. Gladys curtsied.

Henry nodded in acknowledgement and motioned the three to join the others. "We should get down to business. Please everyone, take a seat." He motioned to the table, making his way to the head and sitting, shuffling through the thick folder at his place. "I presume we have most of our issues from the previous meeting settled and the program is coming together without further complications?" It was part statement, part question. Henry took a minute to look around the gathered group of artists, making sure to make eye contact with each one in turn. They all nodded. "Billy. Perhaps you could lead us through the program as it stands now."

"Very well, Your Majesty." Billy cleared his throat. He had been the chair of this committee for a couple of years and even though he was an artist and free spirit at heart, he knew how to handle the business side of anything. Part of the reason why he was so successful with his own art was his proficiency as a good businessman. A salesman too.

The next hour passed swiftly as they outlined the program and shared comments, as well as suggesting a few changes. The general consensus was this would be the best Edinburgh Arts Festival the country had every hosted. Then again, they always vouched to make the current year the best.

"Gentlemen. Ladies." Henry closed the portfolio before him and stood up to bring the meeting to a close. "Thank you. All of you. For working so diligently on this project. We shall meet again in a month's time. Check with Lord Bothwell as you leave to make arrangements for this final meeting before the festival begins." Everyone stood and bowed their heads in acknowledgement. Henry paused briefly, a thought just popping into his head. "Before we go, there is one other matter I would like you to consider. I have decided to donate Balmoral Castle to the arts committee as an artist retreat. Perhaps we could launch the idea with a prize for a month-long sojourn, an invitation of sorts to someone from each branch of the arts community." He ignored the looks of shock and surprise. If things hadn't transpired the way they had earlier, this might never have happened. Now he wanted nothing more to do with anything which reminded him of his friendship with the English royals. Turning Balmoral over to the arts community was a brilliant idea, one which would compliment his mentor, Prince Albert's memory. The castle was, after all, a work of art in itself. It had great potential. He should have thought of the idea sooner. Oh well. It was out there now.

"And as the final thought to consider, I bid you all good day." Henry marched from the room, satisfied to be leaving the others to finish discussing the issues. Seeing George, he gave a tired smile. "I know. I'm running late. I shall see to the science council right away. Make sure the arts council has a meeting set up for next month."

George nodded and made his way into the receiving room. Henry proceeded across the hall. He had almost reached the door to the drawing room when he heard his name called. Turning, he saw his older self waving for his attention.

EIGHT

"Uncle Harry," he greeted the man. He didn't want to waylay the scientists much longer, but it was obvious his older self had something to share. Something important.

"You must try to discourage the time travel research," the older Henry spoke just loud enough for the king to hear. "It's much too soon and too many mistakes will be made if it progresses as planned. Cecil needs watching. I wouldn't grant him too much trust. And I certainly wouldn't grant him the additional funds he's about to request at this meeting."

"How do you know?" Henry asked and then shook his head. Of course he knew. They were both time travelers, though his older self had a little more experience in the art of time travel than his younger self did. "Very well. I shall take your advice under consideration."

Uncle Harry had an amused look on his face. "I thought you might. There are more important things to spend your money on."

"Like." The king raised an eyebrow of curiosity.

"Like electricity, for one. Making it more affordable and

universally available. Just having electric street lights is not enough. And better water management and distribution."

"As in an advanced indoor plumbing system, one more sophisticated than the old Roman model we're still using."

"Exactly. And the science of agriculture needs more funding. There is a way to eradicate the rotting potatoes which are making people starve in many countries. Scotland needs to be ahead of everyone else in agricultural advancements."

"Good point. Anything else?"

"Yes. Make sure to approve bringing Alexander Graham Bell back to Edinburgh where he belongs. He was born here, after all. His studies in long distance communication are amazing."

"The acoustic telegraph. Yes, I've heard of it. An important development, for sure."

"He's not getting funding elsewhere. Offer it to him and he'll be here. You want to keep his patents in Scotland, lad." Patting the young king on the shoulder, the older man nudged him forward. "Now off you go, young man. Don't keep those scientists waiting. Who knows what mischief they can come up with if left to their own devices, in your drawing room for too long?"

"Exactly." Henry chuckled and opened the door to enter the drawing room.

The men within, and the one lady scientist, stood as he entered. All conversation ceased immediately. Silence ensued until, one by one they bowed, the lady curtsied, and they all greeted him with, "Your Majesty."

"Gentlemen." Henry marched swiftly towards the gathered group. Nodding his head to the single lady scientist, "And, my lady." She returned his smile. Waving his hands, he motioned everyone to be seated and he did the same. "Now. We have a lot to accomplish. Who will go first?"

"We are all here to update you on our progress in various research projects, Your Majesty." The woman took the floor and started the meeting. "I have been working on various agricultural issues, particularly the potato blight which has led so many people around the world to the brink of starvation."

One of the men cleared his throat. "All very fine for a lady scientist, Your Majesty." The man stood, interrupting the woman.

"And you are?" Henry knew the names of everyone present except this man. He couldn't remember seeing this man before. Not at these meetings. Yet he was strangely familiar. "I do believe Lady Mallory had the floor, good sir. Perhaps you should introduce yourself first by apologizing for your rudeness."

The man stuttered, blanched and shuffled on his feet. "Yes, Your Majesty. I do apologize, Lady Mallory." Turning back to the king, he continued. "I am Lord Cecil Stuart, Your Majesty. And I have been researching the powerful possibilities of quantum physics."

The room was suddenly full of shaking heads and signs of disbelief. "He's talking about time travel, Your Majesty," Lady Mallory clarified for the king, her voice clearly indicating her distaste for both the man and his research.

Henry cleared his throat. No one present knew of his own personal ability to travel through time, so he chose his words carefully. "And how do you propose the furthering of your research project, Lord Stuart? Another Stuart. Are we related?"

"Perhaps distantly, Your Majesty," Cecil replied briskly. "The entire project is based on principals of wormholes and..."

He didn't get to finish. The woman did it for him. "He wants to implant things into our heads to allow us to jump through time. He claims if we can go back in time, we can change things for the better."

"Or for the worse," Lord Stanley added. "Changing time is a

waste of time, if you ask me and ignore the pun." Lord Robert Stanley was the scientist working on electrical currents, among other things.

"Perhaps." Henry gave a noncommittal response. He waved Cecil to sit, before returning his attention to Lord Stanley. "Robert. We need to invite Alexander to return to Edinburgh, don't you think." Henry used given names for those he had known since childhood. The boys had studied and played together. Henry had always marvelled at their brilliant minds, wishing he understood half of what they were talking about most of the time. Robert and Alexander had been both friends and competitive colleagues for many years. It was not unexpected Henry's request for Robert to invite Alexander and his acoustic device to Edinburgh would meet with a welcome response. Instead, Robert bristled.

"As you wish, Your Majesty." He didn't say any more, sitting with a bit of huff.

The meeting stretched on longer than Henry would have liked. The scientists argued and stated their cases for more funding. Some, like Lady Mallory and her potato research, received it; others, like Cecil's time travel research, received nothing. There was a mixture of content and disgruntled scientists who bowed to Henry when he brought the meeting to a close and marched out of the room. He made his way directly to his chambers, George following closely on his heels.

"Are they gone?" Henry asked when the doors closed behind him and he felt secure in his own space to speak his mind.

"Yes, Your Majesty." George knew what the king was talking about. "The English royal train crossed the border just over an hour ago. All royals on board. Your wife," he stuttered at the reference to the king's wife, not knowing how to address the now exiled Queen of Scotland. "|Is being safely transported to

Loch Leven Castle and will be locked in the tower upon arrival."

"Very good. Send up some tea and toast. I need some sustenance, but I don't care to eat much. Then make sure no one disturbs me until the morning."

"Yes, Your Majesty." George left, closing the doors quietly behind him.

Henry sat in his comfortable chair by the window, stretched out his legs and dozed off as the twilight of early evening submerged his room gradually into darkness.

.

NINE

Holyrood House, Edinburgh, Sometime in the Future

He has walked through this door many times in his life. Holyrood House. His home in Edinburgh. So different. It is never like this. It appears far away. He walks slowly towards it. Stops. Pivots. Stares at the space.

Sterile.

White.

Bright lights.

He looks towards the window he knows should be just to his right. If it is, it's well covered.

Camouflaged.

His private chambers?

It can't be. It's nothing. Certainly nothing familiar.

Clashes cause him to jump and look the other way.

Towards the door.

Out in the hall.

He follows the sounds, tentatively putting one foot in front of the other. His feet feel like lead. They slide along, almost as if he were dragging them. He reaches for the wall to steady himself. He shouldn't be up and about. Isn't it what they said?

Who said?

Someone said it.

When?

What year is it?

He can't remember.

He's traveled through time before. Many times. But to this time? He wasn't sure.

The door slides open at a mere touch.

Not his door. Different. The doors used to be solid oak, carved from the timber once gracing his land.

He steps through the doorway.

And blinks.

Many times.

The light is like daggers piercing his eyeballs.

The hall is as bright, as white and as sterile as the room he left behind him. The doors on either side are shut, but there are windows. Where once there hung portraits and paintings of landscapes, he notices windows. Instead of admiring works of art, he can look inside each room. It had never been the case before.

Everything was so different. This is, or was, his home. His domain. His kingdom.

Yes. He was right.

He is a king. King of Scotland.

He approaches the first room on the side retaining physical support, his hand still braced on the wall to steady him. He looks in the window. There's a bed. A figure lies under crisp white sheets, monitors beeping all around.

It's a woman. Her great ancestor. At least it looks like her. Only younger than he remembers from his frequent jumps through time.

Mary Elizabeth.

Was she queen at this age?

Or had she yet to claim her throne?

He moves on down the hall. The next room is a hive of activity. As he glances through the window, he sees the figure on the bed, covered in the same crisp white sheets as the woman in the previous room. Monitors beeping. But there are others present. All wearing crisp white lab coats. Some carrying needles, syringes.

There's blood.

And voices.

"Close it up." A man's voice.

"Did it take?" A woman's.

"Too soon to tell."

A woman turns towards the door and sees him staring into the room. She marches over and pulls down a blind. He can no longer see what's going on. But he can hear.

"Who was it?" The man again.

"Young King Henry." A woman.

"He is a difficult patient. You would think by the twenty-fifth century our technology would be sufficient to overcome the brain of a nineteenth century human."

"Can you wipe his memory again?"

Again? Wipe his memory? It doesn't sound good. What's going on here? And why would they want to wipe his memory?

"He's too strong. Too independent. His mind's too powerful."

It was time to retreat. But where? He used to know all the safe places in Holyrood House. Places he could hide and not be found. He and Bertie had discovered them together as children. But he was no longer a child. This was no longer the Holyrood House he knew so well.

His brain fog was clearing; his balance restored. He was able to walk along the hall without bracing himself for support.

Looking into another room, he noticed a prone figure connected to a similar arrangement of beeping monitors. This wasn't good. What was going on?

He should escape. Find an exit. The doors to the outside must be as they were.

No. Looking down at his attire, he realized he was a sight.

All he had on was a hospital gown, a light blue, light weight garment which barely reached his knees.

"Your Majesty." The woman's voice. From the room where they worked on a body. Whose body, he didn't know.

Turning, he realized he was caught. Again.

Why did he think he was caught? Why did his mind flash the word 'again' across his memory banks?

The woman reached him and took his arm. "Your room is down this way."

There would be no escaping this time.

TEN

Balmoral Castle, June 1ˢᵗ, Year of Our Lord 1861

"*Uncle Harry.*" *The boys called out in a chorus of cheerful, yet boisterous voices. There was Bertie, overtly assured of himself at the age of twenty, Alfred, not much younger at seventeen, and Leopold a young boy at only eight. The English princes and himself at sixteen. A self-assured young man who, even at a young age, was fond of his English royal cousins.*

Young Henry was standing beside an older man, Prince Albert, Queen Victoria's prince consort. A bond had established between the two. Albert had taken a liking to the young Scottish king, taking him under his wing, so to speak, after Henry's father passed away suddenly when the young prince was only ten. Now at sixteen, he was a young man ready to take on his crown, a task he was determined to do as soon as he was eighteen. In the meantime, the young king was active in his realm.

This latest project, the building of Balmoral, had caused some conflict between himself and his mother, the Regent. Prince Albert had come to his defense, pointing out it would be a great learning project for the king-in-waiting, one his sons would benefit from as well.

As if his thoughts could speak volumes, Albert met his gaze. "Uncle Harry," he called in greeting, a huge smile plastered across his face. He chose to call him uncle to avoid confusion between the other Henry present. "Come see what we're doing."

Henry, the boy, waved him closer. "Uncle Albert has been studying my drawings and he thinks we can use some of my ideas in the castle we're building." He recalled the affectionate title they attributed to Queen Victoria's husband. He had always been such a friendly sort, reaching out to the young people with care and enthusiasm, often treating them as his equal.

When the older Henry stood next to his younger self, he studied the drawings he remembered making all those years ago. "Yes," he agreed with enthusiasm. "I think there should be a tower or two. You have the right idea, young Henry."

"I am not so young, any more, Uncle Harry." The boy took in a deep breath and shook his head, tut-tutting as if scolding his older self. "I will soon be a real king, ruling on my own." At the moment, Henry, the king-in-waiting, demonstrated his true colors. His strengths. His commanding presence. At the moment, he was every inch the king he would soon become.

"Henry. Show your elders some respect." A woman slid towards them, silently. Slid is the best way to describe the manner in which the Regent Queen moved. Everything about her was slick and slippery. You never knew where you stood in her presence and her sharp tongue was always at the ready. The older Henry recognized her conniving personality now, but in his youth, he merely cowered in her presence.

"Elizabeth." Uncle Harry greeted the woman.

She nodded in response. "Henry. I didn't know you were visiting again." She put added emphasis on the word, 'again'. "I have been doing my research. I can't seem to find you in any of my husband's family trees. How did you say you were related?"

"I didn't." He no longer cowered when she challenged. Uncle

Harry met his mother's scrutiny with equal intensity. "Perhaps you should consider some of the illegitimate possibilities?" This woman was being far too analytical of his presence and his right to be with the royals. A simple word explaining his family connection would no longer suffice. A suggestion of an illegitimate drop of royal blood might do. For now.

She tipped her nose in a snub. "Perhaps." She took up position on the other side of young Henry, pretending to show interest in his drawings. "Well, Albert." She ignored her son and addressed the Prince Consort. "What do you think of this project? Truthfully, now. Is this a project worthy of all the time and money?"

"Worthy?" Albert cocked an eyebrow. He was familiar with Elizabeth's challenging ways. Challenging, of course, was a mild description. Elizabeth was every bit her father, Lord George Borthwick, the twenty-second peer of Borthwick Castle in the historic county of Midlothian just south of Edinburgh. One of the oldest royal lords in Scotland, the Borthwick peerage dated its presence in Scotland to the eleventh century when the noble family accompanied Queen Margaret to Scotland during the reign of King Malcolm III. The Borthwick family had long been ardent supporters of the Scottish crown and sided with Queen Mary I as she fled captivity in 1567 and later with her daughter, Queen Mary Elizabeth I, in her claim to the throne which kept the country free and independent. Since then, the Borthwicks enjoyed a rare and honored connection with the royal Stuarts of Scotland, including young Elizabeth's marriage to King James VIII. Henry was their only child, his parents choosing to lead separate lives after his birth. When James was killed tragically in a riding accident, which Henry continued to believe was more than just an accident, Elizabeth was quick to assume the role of Regent of Scotland, a role her family supported. The Borthwick *lust for power and control became exceedingly evident as the young king slowly approached the age of majority, the age when he would assume the throne in his own right.*

Albert was well read in the histories of both England and Scotland. He knew the Borthwick heritage. He recognized their lust for power. Their ability to plot and manipulate others to their own purposes. They were all strong willed, determined people, intent on bending the will of others to mirror their own. They were privileged peers, always close to the Scottish crown, and the first to take advantage of any given situation. When it was decided Henry's father, King George, needed a wife to provide an heir, it was decided a Scottish lass should be chosen. What better choice than a Borthwick lass like Elizabeth.

She was as strong willed and unrelenting in her prejudices and opinions as all the other Borthwicks as well as being a beautiful woman. She hid her obstinate nature from the king until he was pledged to her. She provided him with a son and then sought refuge in her own affairs until the sad demise of Henry's father. Then Elizabeth, Queen and Regent, rose to her full potential. She was a powerful, obstinate force to be reckoned with.

Young Henry couldn't wait to have full control of his realm. Always a patient man, his younger self was quickly losing it where his mother was concerned. He would be a powerful king in his own time, the older Henry gave a smile of satisfaction as he studied his own inner conflict where his mother was concerned. He might be short in patience, but he knew how to avoid confrontation, diplomatically, of course. It was something he honed to perfection, even more so where it concerned his southern neighbors. He was forever aware of the consequences of creating friction between England and Scotland.

"Your son is a good student," Albert gave the regent queen a warm smile. He was also aware of the woman's lust for other

women's husbands. Albert had often been confronted with her uncomfortable advances. So far, he had managed to escape unscathed and with his reputation as a faithful husband to Queen Victoria still intact. "He is learning more than just architecture, dear queen. He is learning to do more than just dream, to see a project through to completion, to find ways to overcome obstacles and to treat his workers fairly. The latter is most important. For we are all God's creatures, equal in His eyes. And we deserve equal respect for our labors."

Elizabeth harrumphed as elegantly as a lady of her stature could. She did not agree with Albert's view of the world. Her greed allowed her only one vision: one of power and control. Giving into worker's rights and demands was definitely not on her agenda. "So you say. No need to preach. I get enough religion every Sunday at church." She patted her son on the shoulder. "Well, Henry. I think you've had enough of building castles for one day. You have other things to consider. Isabel will be arriving soon. You need to make her feel welcome. She will make a good partner for you."

Isabel. The older Henry cringed. He had tried to appease his mother in so many ways. Isabel had been one of those appeasements. One he would regret for as long as she, Isabel, lived. Fortunately, his mother had passed away soon after his marriage to Isabel. Elizabeth no longer presented a problem. Only when he jumped back in time and she challenged his right to claim a connection to the royal family.

Isabel. She was sweet. She was also young. Only thirteen years to Henry's seventeen. She hadn't won his heart yet. His heart belonged to another. Always would. Isabel was still too much a child. But she loved to try. Eventually she would reel him in like a coddled fish. He could tolerate her then, be friendly to her. When she was sixteen. Sweet and innocent. He was blinded *by youth and duty. He did try to appease her ever wish, every desire. He did try to love her.*

It only made her ultimate deception, her spying for England, more painful to endure.

ELEVEN

Holyrood House, Edinburgh, Sometime in the Future

"Your Majesty. You need to rest." The woman again.

He blinked his eyes at the bright lights overhead. "Where am I? What are you doing to me?"

"Nothing you need to worry about."

"And the others?" His eyes darted around the room, trying to take in his surroundings. The light was blinding. His eyes couldn't focus. Even the woman standing over him was a blur of white and skin tones. She was holding something thin and narrow, pointing upwards. Something squirted out. She tapped it with a finger.

"What others?" Her question sounded programmed. A deterrent from what was happening around him. What was happening? He was so confused. Why couldn't he wrap his brain around this place? This event? It was as if his mind was engulfed in a thick fog. He spoke without understanding. He so much wanted to understand.

"Princess Mary Elizabeth. Her mother, Marie de Guise. William Shakespeare of all people. Those others. I know there are more."

"Never you mind," the woman tut-tutted. The hand holding the pointed object lowered. Out of his vision. "You will soon forget."

"I don't want to forget. I want to know. I want to understand." His head spun left. Then right. Then left again. He could feel the constraints. He tried to pull up his arms. He tried to move his legs. He was strapped down. Confined. "Why?" he cried out in frustrated agony. "Why? Why? Why?" His voice cracked as if he was sobbing from deep within. He didn't like this feeling of confinement. He was a man who expected full control over all he did. He was incapable of doing anything at the moment. Except cry out in desperation.

No sympathy from the woman. Just strict words of protocol. "Doctor's orders, Your Majesty. Doctor's orders." A needle pricked his arm. Blackness overtook him. Again.

TWELVE

Holyrood House, Edinburgh, May 1st, Year of Our Lord 1875

Henry left his chambers and immediately went to the nursery. He wanted to make sure his son was safe. He should have checked sooner, but with all the demands on his time and presence, his day had not been his own. The plotting and mischief behind his back plagued him. He couldn't be too careful. He would have to select new nursery staff as the current women employed in this task had been hired by his wife and were, no doubt, faithful to her and not to him.

He didn't knock. He marched through the door. It was his right. There was a flurry of activity in the several rooms set aside for his son's care. The women were packing baby items into trunks with quick efficiency.

"What's this?" he demanded. "What do you think you are doing?"

Everyone froze. They hadn't heard him enter, but they heard him now.

Miss Margaret, young Edward's nanny, made her way to the king and gave him his due reverence with a brisk curtsy. "Your Majesty. We didn't expect you here. We heard the queen had been moved to Loch Leven Castle and we were preparing to join her. The young prince is asleep. Perhaps you would care to see him before we depart?"

"Depart?" Henry bellowed. "You and my son are not going anywhere!"

"But Your Majesty," Miss Margaret stuttered. "I thought..."

He quickly raised a hand to interrupt. "You are in my employ, not the queen's. My son stays here. Now. Start unpacking everything and return these rooms to proper order. Yes, I will check on my son. And I will stay here with him until new staff, people who are loyal to me, can be assigned to replace the lot of you." He waved off any protest and marched through to the next room where young Edward was indeed sound asleep in his cradle.

"Well, my lad." He spoke soothingly to his sleeping son. "It's just you and me, now. Just you and me. Two men at the helm and no conniving, plotting females to hinder our lives. Just the way it should be, don't you think?"

"Your Majesty," Miss Margaret whispered from the door to the adjoining room. "Might I have a word?"

He waved her in. "I will not leave him." He eyed the woman warily. "Anyone complicit in stealing him away shall be charged with treason as well as kidnapping. My son stays with me."

"Yes, Your Majesty. I was misinformed. Please accept my apologies."

Henry merely nodded. "For now. We shall see."

"The others, too. They were only doing as they were told."

"Yes, I suppose they were. Now they must answer to me and only to me."

"Yes, Your Majesty." He reached into the cradle and ever so gently picked up his sleeping son. The baby gurgled and let out a tiny sigh, but otherwise was undisturbed as his father tucked him into the cradle of his arm. Henry couldn't help but smile down at his son as he ran a finger along the infant's chin. As he started to rock the sleeping babe in his arm, he glanced at the nanny. "There are rooms next to mine. We shall set up the nursery there."

"But Your Majesty," Miss Margaret started to protest.

Henry cut her off with a piercing look. "And he is to remain close to me at all times during the day and night. I will be checking on him frequently. And I will be inserting some of my own trustworthy people to attend to his needs. For now, you may keep your job. But be forewarned, Miss Margaret, my eyes are on you. I will make sure you and everyone else around my son are closely watched."

"Yes, Your Majesty." The nanny curtseyed, ducking her head in compliance, though probably hiding her look of discomfort in the process. She walked out briskly, leaving her charge in his father's care.

"Yes, little one," Henry spoke quietly to his son. "We must stand by each other. It's just the two of us, now. You and me against the world."

THIRTEEN

Loch Leven Castle, Late Autumn, Year of Our Lord 1875

"You came," Isabel remained seated by the fire. She was wrapped in multiple layers of shawls and blankets in an attempt to look feeble and frigid cold. *Frigid, yes,* the king thought to himself. *But cold?* Well, he supposed it was a little cold in this stone tower. "Did you bring our son?"

"No." His answer was abrupt. He had steeled himself for the visit, one she had demanded on many occasions. She had threatened all manner of things to get him to come. When she had managed, well almost, to escape the castle, as had his predecessor several generations earlier, he had taken it upon himself to make sure the castle tower was reinforced. He had brought an entirely new contingent of guards and personal attendants for the queen. It was bad enough she had managed to weave a web a deceit to entrap his once close friend and trusty confidante, George. Her sneaky ability to enlist the help of others at the castle and almost make a successful escape, all with the intent of kidnapping his son on their way out of the country, made her look even more pitiful. She had even planned to seek refuge in England.

She moved slightly to allow herself a look at her husband, the king. "Why not? He is my son."

"I don't want your influence to tarnish his innocence. You have managed to turn others against me. You even managed to get yourself with child, not by me, and to have the child while trying to pass him off as mine son and heir. To make matters worse, it appears you have used my cousin, no less, as the boy's real father." He studied her closely. In the dim light with only the flames in the hearth to brighten the room, it was difficult to tell if she were pregnant. Then again, she had been late to show with Edward. "I wonder," he tapped his chin thoughtfully. "Are you with child? Again. Another child fathered by someone other than your own husband."

She diverted the question and cocked a half smile. "Poor George. He didn't know what happened until it was over."

Shaking his head in disgust. "You're a witch. If you had lived a hundred years ago, I would have had you burned at the stake."

She cackled a laugh to suit her case. "Oh well! So, will you claim this child as yours?" She patted her belly, which betrayed nothing. "Only a few months to go."

"No. But I won't allow you or your allies to have it either. As soon as it's born, if it's born as I highly doubt there is a babe within you, I will have it brought to the royal nursery to be raised as Edward's half-sibling. I might give it a title. It remains to be seen." He broke his gaze from the woman he had been forced to love, to pledge his life to, focussing instead on the flames flickering in the fireplace.

A silence enveloped the chasm between them. She broke it first. With accusation, of course. "You have cut off my correspondence. I receive no news from my family in London. Why?" Her eyes pleaded her cause. It had no effect, as he continued to stare at the flames.

"You continue to plot against me. Simple as that."

"So, you change the locks. Change the guards. Change my personal attendants. And you deny me access to my son and, once this child is born, you will deny me access to him or her as well. I may as well lose my head as stay confined like this for eternity."

"You made your own bed, Isabel." He stole a glance at her, his eyes brittle like ice. "If you had been satisfied just being my wife and the mother of our children, you wouldn't be here. Instead, you had to align yourself with the greed of the English royal family."

"Greed? It's not greed. It's practical sense." She spat at him. "But you are too close-minded in your thinking to realize it. Bigger countries are stronger countries."

"We already are one of the strongest countries in the world," he argued vehemently and with deep passion. "Aligning our empire with the English would only benefit the English. We are Scottish and only Scottish."

"Oh, yes! I know!" She managed a sneer before he could steal his eyes away and look into the flames again. "For now and forever. Your age-old battle cry." She snorted in disgust. "Times are changing, Henry. It's time you realized bigger is better."

"I will prove you wrong, Isabel. You and the English, and the entire world for that matter. Bigger is not always better." He swung on his heel and stomped out of her chambers, the room at the top of the tower where Queen Mary had once plotted her own battles. Perhaps he should reconsider her imprisonment at Loch Leven. There must be other castles, more isolated and more secure. He would think on it. For now, though he couldn't escape fast enough. He cringed at the thought he once dreamed of living his life and ruling his realm with this woman. Now though, he couldn't stand to be near her for mere minutes.

She called out to him, but he didn't pause. He had put off

this visit for months. After discovering George blinded by her pleas and seductive advances, he knew he had to investigate the lodgings, the security and make some changes in the people who took care of his wife and guarded her. He had selected two women to care for her. She didn't need more. He was paying well for the ladies' loyalty to him. They would work as attendants for Isabel and spies for Henry. In return, they would receive a large enough dowry after two years of service which would ensure an arranged marriage to a high-ranking noble was within their grasp. The women came from large families, lesser nobles, with aspiring hopes to move up on the noble ladder of success. The women were told, quite bluntly, do their jobs with care and remain loyal to the king and they would achieve added prosperity, not just for themselves, but also for their families. Should they be deceived by Isabel and plot against the king, then their families would all suffer. His promises coupled with threats was enough to put the fear of God and king in their hearts. They would not fail.

As for the men on guard, he chose brothers of the women who served Isabel. He ordered no one, man or woman, should be left alone with Isabel. His wife's privacy was no longer an issue, as far as he was concerned. If one of the guards needed an audience with Isabel, then he would attend her chambers accompanied by another guard as well as both women attendants.

The final terms he set down regarded visitors to Loch Leven and correspondence. There would be neither. All her meals would be searched for hidden notes before she was served. Her laundry and personal items would also be searched before given to her. The only visitor allowed was himself.

It was cruel, but necessary. Isabel had cornered herself into this sad situation. She would have to bear the consequences.

As he left the chambers, he cranked the newly installed

lock, ensuring its security. He had inspected all the windows during the brief visit, visually assessing their installation. He wasn't too worried about Isabel trying to escape through the windows, as they were small enough to make squeezing through difficult, especially in the garments the former queen continued to insist on wearing. There was also a sharp, steep drop from the windows, landing on the rocky shore of the loch. Unless Isabel miraculously grew her hair as long as the fairy tale princess, Rapunzel, there was little chance of a successful escape through the windows.

He could hear his former partner calling in despair as he trotted down the stairs and out the final door. He checked the lock on this door as well. Satisfied all was secure, he shared a few words with the captain of the guard before stepping into the rowboat which would take him back to the mainland.

Henry was deep in thought as the boat rocked gently across the water to the main shore. He was anxious to return to Holyrood, to make sure his son was safe. He was always nervous leaving him behind for official functions and visiting Isabel was no different. It could be a ploy. The nightmare had plagued him all day and for days leading up to this journey. He recalled the young King James VI being kidnapped frequently before he was of age to assume his throne. He didn't want the same horrors to besiege his son's young years.

FOURTEEN

Toronto, Canada, Summer, Year of Our Lord 2016

The humidity hit him first. It was like a wall of suffocation smacking him hard in the face every which way he moved. With his heavy garments, long sleeved shirt and wool jacket over wool pants, he felt like he was melting. The sweat dribbled relentlessly carving a path of wet destruction under his arms, down his back and even down his legs. It was uncomfortable, to say the least.

"Not the best place for your attire," a voice noted from behind him. Henry thought he recognized the voice, but he couldn't place it. He moved to meet his commentator face-to-face. "Never felt heat and humidity like this before, I'll wager."

Henry shook his head. "No, I haven't."

"Well, Your Majesty. Welcome to Toronto in July, a time when you can fry eggs on the sidewalk in less than a minute." The man held out his hand. Henry took it and shook it. He didn't know what else to do. This was unfamiliar territory to him and the few people who walked around him had nothing but strange looks directed at him. Even the landscape was bizarre. Hard stone slabs pushed volumes of heat through his feet and up his legs. Tiny quarters of lush grass, neatly trimmed

and lined with colorful flower beds. Buildings of brick and wood.

He studied his surroundings and then returned his gaze to the man. "You know me and yet I can't place you."

"James Stuart, Your Majesty. The year is 2016 and you are in Toronto, standing outside Marie de Guise's twenty-first century house." He pointed across the street to a grand mansion, of sorts. At least a house bigger than the others around it, but certainly not of the scale he was used to in Scotland. "Your many great grand-mother and her daughter, the Princess Mary Elizabeth. Both of them will soon be returning to their time in the sixteenth century, a time when the princess awaits the death of the English queen so she can take her place, her true place, in Scottish history, as Queen of Scotland." He paused to let his words sink in, then continued, "but not until I've had a chance to talk to them first. You're welcome to join me as I lead her into and out of trouble." He quirked an eyebrow. Henry shook his head. "You're right. Probably not a good idea. Yet. The princess still doesn't quite understand who she is and where she belongs. But she will. Soon. Just in time to make her daring escape and to see her mother, Mary Queen of Scots, for the first time."

"Unbelievable," Henry muttered under his breath.

"Real heady stuff as they would say in the twenty-first centu-ry." James chuckled and fondly slapped Henry on the back. "We have met, you know. I was at your son's christening. You might want to take a page out of Marie de Guise's notebook on how to protect a child who may one day rule."

He didn't wait for an answer and he didn't offer further explanation. With a smart bow, he crossed the street, leaving Henry standing, bewildered, not quite knowing what to do or what James meant by his suggestion.

He stood and watched as the young princess answered the door, looking every bit like a common servant girl. From what *little he could see, she was even dressed in the garb of the ordinary Scottish working girl, one who worked the fields, not in a grand house. Why would a princess answer the door?*

James walked in without a backward glance and the door closed behind him. Without further thought, Henry trotted across the hard, concrete surface which he assumed to be the roadway. A horn honked at him and he jumped with fright when he noticed a large, horseless carriage, or so he thought, barrelling towards him. He quickened his pace.

He trotted up the front steps as noiselessly as possible and made his way to the front door. Should he knock? Announce himself? Enter into the foray, such as it was? Voices came from the other side. He strained to listen, following them as they seemed to move to a room behind the window to his right. He moved over to listen more closely.

A woman's voice, an exceptionally commanding voice, came across brilliantly clear. He couldn't see through the windows with the curtains drawn, but he was sure it was the voice of Marie de Guise, Mary Elizabeth's grandmother. "You have no right to call me by my given name, in this century or in the past. Now state your purpose."

"My purpose has always been the same." It was James's voice. Henry couldn't be sure, but he believed James was the only male in the house. "Marie. Or should I be addressing you as Your Majesty?"

"What's he talking about, Grandmother?" Mary Elizabeth. He would recognize her voice anywhere. After many visits with his many great grandmother, both in her time and in his, he knew he wasn't mistaken. Mary Elizabeth had a charming quality to her voice. Soft, like a touch of velvet, forceful only when needed. "Why does he call you Marie? And Your Majesty?"

"She doesn't know, does she?" James could be heard pacing

the room and slapping his side to accentuate his words. "Well I'll be..."

"No swearing in this house." A warning issued by Marie de Guise.

"I think you should tell your granddaughter the whole truth." There was a strong sense of determination in James' voice. "If you don't, I will." There was silence. James was pausing for added effect, allowing his words to sink in. "As you wish. Your Gran, as you call her is your grandmother, in both the present and the past, in the sixteenth century. She is Marie de Guise, second wife of King James V of Scotland and mother of Mary Queen of Scots. She was regent during Queen Mary's infancy and died, some say of poison, in 1560. Your mother, my dear Mary Elizabeth, was none other than Mary Queen of Scots herself. You are the twin who lived. It was Mrs. Dickson, the old lady as you called her then, or Mrs. D, as you call her now, who brought you to this time and place and actually saved your life. Because you surely would not have survived another day as a preemie in the sixteenth century." Another pause. "Did I sum things up adequately?"

A pregnant silence followed. Mary Elizabeth broke it first. "Gran, is it true? Is all he says true?"

"Of course, it's true, my dear little princess." James' voice was sounding so uncharacteristically like a snarl. James didn't usually snarl. At least, he never had on the few times Henry recalled meeting him. For he did recall him now. At the christening at least. "I should add, my dear cousin, we are related, but not quite the way you have surmised. Yes, the resemblance is uncanny, but then again, the Earl of Moray, James Stuart, your mother's older illegitimate brother, is my blood uncle. I inherited his title. Now, if you haven't already guessed, the real purpose of this little charade involving time travel is to ensure Scotland *never does unite with England. And that, my dear Princess Mary Elizabeth, is where you come in."*

"Me?" Her voice was a squeak.

The next part of the conversation was drowned out by several large horseless vehicles roaring down the road behind him. When all was silent again behind him, Henry was able to hear Mary Elizabeth ask, in a voice which betrayed a sense of confusion mixed with disbelief. "Is it all true, Gran? How could I be there holding myself as a baby? A person can't exist twice in one time and place, can they?"

"Yes, my child." Marie de Guise's voice hinted at a desperate plea for understanding and compassion. "It is all true, all James told you. I am your real grandmother, the mother of Mary Queen of Scots, who was your mother. You are quite right. One person cannot exist twice for an extended period of time, in one time, but this was an anomaly because you had just been born and were not quite living yet. And if my dear friend here, who you fondly refer to as Mrs. D, had not taken you from that time and place and brought you to the present time, you would probably not be living then or now. Preemies did not live long in the sixteenth century, if at all. Mrs. Dickson brought the baby, Princess Mary Elizabeth, you, here to Toronto, and I immediately took you to Emergency at The Hospital for Sick Children to have you admitted into the Neonatal Intensive Care Unit where they placed you in an incubator. They saved your life."

"But how did you explain it to the authorities? I know I have a Canadian birth certificate, but you would have to prove parentage, wouldn't you?" Henry wasn't sure he understood what being a Canadian meant. Not in this twenty-first century. It had only been a few years ago in his time when Scotland's domain of an amalgamated Upper and Lower Canada had started its expansion westward with great fervor. It had created a union of sorts, a country called Canada, but still under the jurisdiction of the

Scottish government. In his era, in spite of this union, people born in Canada were still considered to be Scottish. Not this Canadian notion.

Marie de Guise was explaining herself. "It was not easy, my dear child. Not in the least. I made up a story that I heard whimpering like a kitten outside my back door. When I went to investigate, I found you wrapped in a blanket. The police and children's services became involved, but nothing proved me either right or wrong. I applied to take custody of you and, by the time the courts approved my application, you were old enough, strong enough, and well enough to come home with me. Mrs. Dickson remained here and helped me raise you until you were about two, then she returned to Scotland. It's why you haven't met her before, or at least you don't remember meeting her. She did come to visit on occasion. We both remained in this time, believing it safer until you were old enough to accept your purpose, your true calling, to be the Queen of Scotland the Scottish people of the sixteenth and seventeenth centuries wanted. Needed."

"Whoa! Wait just a minute!" Mary Elizabeth's voice registered shock. "Even if all of this were true and I am Princess Mary Elizabeth, Queen Mary's daughter, there's the little issue about my brother, who was already King James VI of Scotland and later King James I of England and Scotland."

"But, when James moved south and amalgamated his reign to England, the Scots became vassals and slaves of English landlords and were treated harshly and unfairly for generations. All of the history centered around English dominancy can be avoided if another rightful heir, you..." Henry was lost. This was a timeline he didn't know. Mary Elizabeth had changed things. And for the better. "Yes, you, Mary Elizabeth. If you were to take the reins and challenge King James I of England, you could legitimately take the throne of Scotland and keep the country a free nation for future generations."

James cleared his throat, interrupting the women. "Then we wouldn't have this blasted ongoing conflict and demands to separate from England. We could rule our people, our way, and decide for ourselves whether or not we want to remain in the European Union." Another concept Henry didn't understand. As long as he maintained Scotland's independence, he shouldn't have to concern himself with the issues James was suggesting existed in this alternate timeline.

Another vehicle came down the road. A long, dark, slick railway car sized vehicle. At least in length. The windows were shut and tinted black. It was moving slowly. Towards the house. Henry had a bad feeling about this. It was time to make his exit. As he recalled from Mary Elizabeth's journals as well as Marie de Guise's journals, this was the time when all hell broke lose for the Scottish royals. This house would be a victim along with anyone in or near it, if he didn't make a hasty exit.

FIFTEEN

Scotland Wilds, Autumn, Year of Our Lord 1875

The ride was hard. Henry preferred his horse to a carriage jostling around on uneven ground. Although he had encouraged and helped finance the construction of better roads through the country, the heavy rains this year in particular had rutted each road with great cavities, there being little left to truly call a road. He never had cared for riding carriages, resorting to the uncomfortable mode of conveyance only when protocol dictated. Besides, this was faster. He could cut across the countryside to make better time.

Henry knew the lay of the land. He rode this terrain frequently in his youth. Up and down the burghs and across the open fields, crashing through thick layers of forest growth, scattering birds and animals of all sizes in the wake of his thunderous assault. He knew where to tread carefully. The slopes would be most slippery after the heavy rains. He didn't want to risk his horse. A slip could break a leg which would mean the painful end of a precious animal.

He thundered along, his escorts struggling to keep pace. It was imperative he make good time, imperative he return to his son before it was too late. Something was making him feel unsettled. He didn't know what it was, but he had an inkling something wasn't right. His son wasn't safe.

He also understood the importance of protecting himself, to avoid unexpected ambushes along the way. Hence the armored escorts, trusted men who knew the terrain as well as he did. He would have preferred riding alone. It certainly would have been quicker. For his own safety, however, he had to take the necessary precautions. At all times. It wasn't just his son's life which was in constant jeopardy. His was as well.

He was determined, however, to make good time returning to Edinburgh. This niggling thought about something being amiss plagued his mind. If he didn't make it by nightfall, he would puddle jump, as his great ancestor had jokingly called it, to check on Edward's safety and well being.

"Your Majesty," Robbie called from just behind him. They had reached a flat stretch of land stretching for miles. Robbie, or more correctly, Lord Robert MacDuff, was another childhood friend and trusted confidante. After George's deception and affair with Isabel, Henry had become closer to Robbie. "We should make camp. Stop for the night."

Henry pulled up his horse, allowing Robbie to ride up beside him. He surveyed the land ahead, knowing full well dangers still awaited, dangers which in daylight were bad enough, but after dark, they were downright deadly. "You're right, Robbie. Right as always."

"We can take refuge in the caves over yonder," Robbie waved a hand off to the right. "We used them as children. Remember?"

"Aye. Good idea. Lead on."

The steady plop of the horse's hooves as the animal slopped through mud and puddles had a calming effect. Henry's horse followed Robbie's lead while Henry's mind wandered. It often did whenever he was trying to calm his nerves, as he was now. If Edward was in danger, Henry would find out soon enough. As soon as the camp settled for the night, he would make his jump. He urgently needed to travel through time, not too far. His son was in danger and if he waited for the morrow to reach Edinburgh, it might be too late. He had to make sure his son was safe. Rescue him if need be.

As they plodded slowly up the thickly overgrown path to the caves of their childhood games, Henry recalled some of his many experiences as a time traveler. This gift of shifting through time portals, if it's what they were, had been beneficial as well as, at times, dangerous. He recalled his first jump. He had been ten or so at the time. His tutor had been intent on teaching him the rudiments of Scottish history and they were at the point where he was reading with passionate interest about his great ancestor, Mary Queen of Scots and her daughter, Queen Mary Elizabeth. One night, still awake after the candles had been snuffed, Henry was allowing his mind to go through the events leading up to Mary Elizabeth's claim to the Scottish throne. All of a sudden, he was there. Or, at least, he was in the midst of a crucial moment in her early life.

SIXTEEN

Greenwich Castle, Summer, Year of Our Lord 1587

Squished between nobles dressed in their heavily jeweled and fur-covered robes, Henry, tall for his young age, could just barely see above the shoulders of those in front of him. Just as well he was inconspicuous. Henry, the lad, was after all, dressed in only his night clothes. Certainly not suitable attire for a royal gathering, which is what he assumed he was witnessing. He heard some gasps behind him, and some whispers about his appearance, but nothing to concern himself about. At least, not yet.

Young Henry didn't notice the older Henry, as king, dressed in his muddy riding attire standing nearby, witnessing his first jump back in time.

King Henry watched as his younger self craned his neck to see none other than Queen Elizabeth I on her throne, holding court. It had to be her. The wig, the white powdered face, the heavy assortment of jewels and the richly brocaded gown. He recalled the awe he felt then and couldn't help but feel again.

"Your Majesty." The room was eerily silent as the announce-ment was made from the far end. All heads pivoted in the general

direction. Watched and listened. "Her Royal Highness, the Princess Mary Elizabeth of Scotland, daughter of the late Queen Mary of Scotland and her husband, Lord Bothwell, granddaughter of James V of Scotland and his wife, Marie de Guise. Cousin of our Queen, Elizabeth I of England. Accompanied by her royal entourage."

Gasps fluttered through the room and a path opened up like the Red Sea in the story of Moses leading the Israelites from Egypt. There she was.

Both Henry's watched in awe, the others equally enraptured, as Princess Mary Elizabeth gracefully placed one foot in front of the other, her tiny silk slippers peaking through the hemline of her dress. White and full in its bountiful layers of silk and lace, the dress swished in time to her pace. The long train of the rich deep blue velvet cloak pulled gracefully on the floor rushes behind her.

The walk itself was obviously a difficult one, but the princess kept her steely eyes glued to the target, the English queen. Henry's eyes stole a look towards Queen Elizabeth, witnessing her stone-faced stance as she observed the proceedings with an icy welcome. However, she did return the princess's gaze with equal furor, matching it with a note of respect.

The procession was slow, measured, each footstep executed with precision. The gaze locked between princess and queen never wavered. Princess Mary Elizabeth reached the raised dais on which sat the English queen. She paused and then performed a most elegant curtsy. Henry, in all his ten years in the Scottish royal court, had never seen anything so beautiful. It was the moment he felt his chest burst with pride for his great ancestor.

"Your Majesty," the princess paid her respects in a loud, clear voice, laced with both grace and conviction. More softly, she added the words, "Cousin."

Queen Elizabeth noticeably grimaced at Mary Elizabeth's

final greeting. "How dare you!" she snarled between clenched teeth. It would appear the princess's presence was trying Queen Elizabeth's infamous temper to its limits. Young Henry gaped, mouth wide open, eyes bulging with surprise. Henry, the king, had to stifle a chuckle, not just at his younger self's reaction, but because he had been here before, witnessing this act. "How dare you come here and claim to be a princess of Scotland and my cousin?" She waved her hand imperiously, almost violently so, in front of Mary Elizabeth's face.

"I dare," the princess answered, keeping her voice calm, measured. "Because I was born with the right to dare. When all the forces of England and Scotland would have seen me dead at birth, I have risen above their most awesome powers and have come to claim my rights."

King Henry's smile broadened with pride and a deep, long held respect. He had learned a lot from this woman over the years. All his visits to her in the past and with her in his time had been educational. She had been instrumental in making him the strong king he was in his time. He knew he was a strong king. A good king. The strength of his nation, his people, was evidence of this simple fact.

"Your rights?" The queen glowered. Her heavily powdered face was starting to crumble as plumes of white dust fell on her bosom and her shoulders, leaving behind the straining, bulging veins of an angry woman: an angry old woman.

"Yes, my rights." Mary Elizabeth matched her glare with the queen's, tilting her nose slightly upwards as if she were regally looking down upon someone of lesser importance. "I am Princess Mary Elizabeth of Scotland, daughter of Queen Mary of Scotland, your cousin, the one you murdered!"

The silence in the room couldn't be more overwhelming. Everyone waited. Even the gasps which would normally follow such an abrasive comment were held in check. The queen also waited, her pallor bleached whiter than the powder flattering off her cheeks. Eyes locked on each other, there was a battle of wills at play and whoever blinked first would lose.

"So, you claim." The queen waved her hand dismissively as if the princess's declarations were frivolous and of no importance. "If it were so, if you were the princess born to Queen Mary at Loch Leven Castle, then where have you been all these years? And how is it the queen's gaoler at the time and her half-brother, James Stuart, Earl of Moray and Regent of Scotland, could not find any evidence of a baby's existence after the queen's long labor giving birth? Can you explain it for me?"

"I was overseas," Mary Elizabeth answered quite honestly. Her voice rather polite as if she were shrugging off accusations. "My mother gave me to a trusted servant just after I was born, to ensure I wouldn't be handily disposed of, or worse, made a prisoner of the realm like she was and like my brother, the King of Scotland, was during his childhood. And then there were all those attempted kidnappings of my brother. I wonder who had planned them. And, if the world had known I existed, would I have been used as a similar pawn of politics?"

The queen blanched at the princess's mention of the many failed attempts to kidnap King James VI of Scotland. Henry the lad was mesmerized by the ongoing battle of wits. King Henry was revisiting his knowledge of the past, knowing full well Queen Elizabeth, though she claimed ignorance to these plots, was complicit in both the kidnapping plots and Queen Mary's execution.

Times never changed. Subterfuge and espionage between royal courts was still rampant in his time. Which was why he had to return to his son quickly. To protect him at all cost.

SEVENTEEN

Scotland Wilds, Autumn, Year of Our Lord 1875

He was jostled back to his time as if he had awakened from a sleep-induced coma. Henry had just revisited his first jump. It had been unsettling to see himself as a lad, witnessing a turning point in English and Scottish history. He must have been tired to shuffle through time while traversing the wilds of Scotland on horseback with an armored guard. He glanced around, but no one seemed to notice anything unusual about him or their surroundings. He hadn't been found out.

He shook his head to clear the cobwebs. Robbie was dismounting before a dark opening in the side of the mountain, the path they had climbed ended abruptly at a somewhat level clearing. The mist which had plagued them from Loch Leven was thickening into an intense fog. As darkness fell, the light dwindled to next to nothing. It would be suicide to try riding further through this. Any able Scotsman knew the risks of traveling through dense fog in the highland wilderness, especially at night.

"We'll make camp here," Robbie instructed the men. He

glanced at the king, who nodded in agreement and started to dismount.

Henry gave his horse a fond pat and led him to the trees where two of the guard had already set up a line to tether the horses. He proceeded to untack his mount, content to do the task others would deem below the rank of a king. Caring for his horse helped to bond with him. There were times and dangerous situations when a rider needed to feel connected to his mount. What better way to make this connection than to show some care and affection for the animal? Tethered and untacked, Henry took additional time to rub down his horse. They had paused briefly at the stream to water their horses before starting the climb. There was sufficient greenery to feed the horses within reach of the tethered line. They would receive a good feeding of oats once they returned to Holyrood House on the morrow. Henry would insist.

Satisfied his mount was secure for the night, he made his way into the cave where the others were working to get a fire started near the opening. He pitched in. There was only minimal chatter. Everyone was exhausted from the day's ride. They worked as a team, each one seeming to know what was expected and executing their tasks without complaint.

As Henry helped set up the campsite inside the cave, he allowed the silence to ease his thoughts as he continued to reflect on some of his other jumps through time. The secrets he learned each jump, the privileged information helped him execute a good decision when ruling his domain. He remembered waking the morning after his first jump. He recalled the confusion, wondering if he should tell anyone, realizing no one would believe him. He had told Bertie. Once. Bertie had laughed at him. Bertie didn't believe him. He called his adventures a fantastic dream and frequently teased him whenever they were together.

"Any more dreams of different times, Cousin?" Bertie would snicker, not afraid to share his teasing with whomever was present.

"No dreams, Cousin. Just reality." Henry developed a plausible response for each occasion. Gradually Bertie's teasing evaporated as the desired response was never what he expected.

Secrets.

Lots of secrets.

Past and future secrets, of a time which for him, never stood still.

One of the soldiers returned to the cave bearing a line of fish. "We'll eat well tonight," he called out, dropping his catch by the fire.

Henry hadn't seen the man leave the cave to catch their evening meal. He believed everyone was present and accounted for. He glanced around, counting the heads. There was one more. *Was this soldier, the one with the fish, an imposter? A spy? Friend or foe?* No one else seemed to notice the extra man in the cave. Not even Robbie. Henry found this strange.

As if sensing the king's intensity of a stare, the soldier caught his eye and held the look. They studied each other thoroughly for several minutes. Recognition was slow in coming.

"James," the king whispered, but said no more. It was James Stuart. Here again. *To help him? Or hinder him?*

The man merely nodded then returned to the task of gutting the fish and skewering them on sticks to hang over the fire. *Yes, the men would eat well tonight.*

As the men settled around the fire to enjoy their meal, James made a point of sitting next to the king. "You must go," he whispered as he ate. "Your son is in danger."

Henry nodded. "I expected as much."

"Once they're asleep."

Henry nodded again. Robbie sidled over to the king. "I'll take the first watch, Your Majesty." He pointed to the back of the cave. "It's probably best if you sleep further in the cave. We'll rotate shifts. I'll wake up one of the men to take over."

"You look tired, Sire," James spoke up. "Perhaps I should take the first shift. I can wake you in a few hours to take over."

Henry understood. James taking the watch would mean no one would notice his absence. Only James. The one who understood best about time travel.

Robbie studied the king. Henry nodded. "I think it's for the best, Robbie," he said. "You do look a little peaked. We need you well rested for the morning. Who knows what awaits us in Edinburgh?"

"Very well, Your Majesty." He nodded at James. "Thank you."

It was some time later before Henry felt it safe to make a jump. He was restless as the men lounged around the fire after sharing idle chit chat. Rain had taken over the world beyond the cave, great torrents of water thundering down the slopes, creating a wall, a division, between inside the cave, where it was cozy and warm, and outside.

The long ride had been exhausting and the men finally succumbed to much needed slumber. James took the first watch and Robbie decided to bed down next to Henry. Close to keep his king well protected. How much protection he could offer in this deep slumber, Henry didn't know, but he breathed a sigh of relief when Robbie's loud snores joined the others in the cave. It was a symphony of sounds: the roaring rain outside and the soothing snores inside. As the snores increased in both numbers and volume, Henry curled into his cloak for warmth and feigned sleep, counting quietly to keep his brain active without disturbing the others. With James on watch, for now, it was safe.

He knew all he had to do was think about where he was going. It's what had happened on the ride up the mountain. It would happen the same way again. He never understood how it worked. It just did. Like magic? Or was it?

EIGHTEEN

Holyrood House, Edinburgh, Autumn, Year of Our Lord 1875

He was never sure if he was dreaming or physically present in the alternate time. All he had done was think of his last moments with his son before he left to visit his wife. Suddenly, he was there, behind the drapes in the nursery, watching, absorbing the precious moment which was securely etched in his mind and his heart.

He watched in awe as the memory took life, as he kissed his son's forehead before placing him in the cradle. His other self hesitated, not wanting to leave. But he did, slowly, closing the door quietly behind him.

Henry listened intently to the sounds of his own footsteps receding down the hall. A few moments later, there were shouts and hoof beats clattering through the courtyard below. These, too, diminished in volume. Then silence. He desperately wanted to peak in the cradle. To pick up his son and hold him. To be assured all was well. Something told him to wait.

He slipped further behind the drapes, even though the light was dim, almost dark, the only bright spot being the few sparkling embers in the fireplace.

"In here," Miss Margaret, the nanny called to someone in the adjoining room. The nursery door opened and he watched as Miss Margaret walked into the room motioning someone to follow. "Shh! He's asleep. We must be quiet." Something was amiss. He knew he should never have trusted the woman.

"Get him. We leave now." A coarse voice. Male. Unfamiliar, but definitely English. The accent gave it away. "We must go now. While all's quiet. The sleeping potion will keep the guards out for at least an hour. Not much longer. Hurry up, woman." Impatient. Angry. Abrupt. His voice said it all. A loud voice. And he was a big man. It was evident from the large shadow blocking the light from the other room as the figure filled the door-way. He didn't venture too far into the room. Just as well. He might have seen Henry as he slunk even deeper into the folds of drapery.

"It won't take me long. I have a bag ready." She scurried about the room, returning to the man standing at the door. She handed him the bag. "Wait downstairs. In the courtyard. I'll bring the young prince."

"See that you do!" He snapped and moved away, the bag thrown carelessly over one shoulder.

Henry was unsure what to do. He had to rescue his son. Before it was too late. What had they done to his guards? Drugged them? And what was the plan for the little prince? Other than the obvious: abduction.

His moment of indecision was rewarded when Miss Margaret gasped and said to herself, "Oh, I can't leave without..." The rest was lost as her voice faded away.

It was now or never. Henry pushed away the drapes and almost slid over to the cradle in his haste to move both quickly and quietly. Stealth was of the upmost importance. He scooped up his son and made a beeline back to the drapes.

He knew this place like the back of his hand. All those years as a child, growing up in this rambling, monolithic structure. What else was there for a young prince to do except explore? And explore he did. He knew every hidden recess, secret staircase and unused exits from top to bottom. There was a passage in the corner, behind the drapes, next to the window. It was a narrow staircase spiralling downwards to other rooms below, including his own private chambers, and then to the main floor where it exited into the courtyard. Not the best option at the moment, but the staircase was behind a seldom accessed panel. No one knew about it. No one in this era when the art of espionage didn't necessarily include secret passageways. There were no building floorplans to outline these secrets. They had served a purpose in the past, then had been forgotten over the generations. Until now. Henry knew them. He knew all there was to know. Good thing too.

He found the latch and swung the door open, cringing at the slight squeak. He would have to remember to oil it. No. He wouldn't allow anyone else to do the task. He didn't want anyone else to know of his secret escape routes. He had just slipped into the stairwell and pulled the panel shut until it latched when he heard Miss Margaret's return. It was her scream which carried through the walls.

"He's gone!"

Footsteps thundered, approaching. "What do you mean he's gone?" The man again. Henry was starting to recognize the arrogance which laced the English man's voice. The drapes were slashed back, hands skittered across the surface of the walls beyond the hidden staircase. Henry cuddled his son closer, hoping he wouldn't wake and give them away. He knew he was safe enough, for now, but he had to find a way out of the castle. Henry wasn't sure if he could puddle jump, as his ancestors often called it, to take him into the city where a safe house might be assured for both him and his son. Would the infant prince jump with him? Henry didn't know whether non-time travelers could jump. Then again, the infant Princess Mary Elizabeth, with Marie de Guise's trustworthy lady, had been carried into the future, long before she demonstrated her own unique time traveler abilities. Perhaps it would work.

As if he could conjure the woman into his presence, he heard, "Come. Now." A whispered voice. A woman. It sounded like Marie de Guise. He couldn't see well in the dark space. "Quickly. There isn't much time." Her voice came from below. Beckoning. He had to follow the sound of her voice.

Banging against the wall startled him "There must be a secret passage. Where is it? Where have you hidden the prince?" Tension mounted as the man's temper exploded in thumps and kicks, getting closer by the minute.

"I don't know what you're talking about," the nanny squeaked out an answer. "I've never found any secret passages in this room, though I've heard rumors there are several in the building."

"I don't believe you. When I'm done here, I will take care of you. Guards!" Miss Margaret shrieked as someone obviously grabbed her. The banging intensified. It was now or never.

Henry held the still sleeping baby closer. He moved towards the whispered voice, carefully taking each narrow step, feeling as best he could with his foot each time he descended to the next step. He made it to the landing which he knew was just outside his own chambers.

"Marie de Guise," he greeted his ancestor with whispered reverence.

"Henry. You and your son are in grave danger. Come. We will go to the future where he will be safe in my care until such time as it is safe to return here where he belongs."

"Will it work?" Henry didn't hear an answer. Instead, the

banging from above diminished, replaced by a cacophony of clashing noises of another sort. He opened his eyes.

"Welcome to the twenty-first century." He swung his head back and forth, taking in the marvels of the space around him. Paved roads, horseless carriages, large homes. He remembered this place. Before. He had been here before. The day Mary Elizabeth learned her true calling, her place in Scottish history.

"Welcome to the year of Our Lord, 2018, and to my home in Toronto." Marie de Guise motioned across the street and led the way to a large, Queen Anne style, red-brick house, complete with turrets and pillars to project an image of importance.

Henry followed his great ancestor as she made her way to the house. On closer inspection, he noted the windows were blackened. It hadn't appeared so from across the street, but, the closer he was to the house, the darker they were. Definitely blackened.

"How do you look out?" he asked, indicating the windows with one hand.

"We have peep holes here and there." Marie spoke in little more than a whisper. Putting her finger to her lips, she suggested silence. "We're not safe until we're inside. Too many spies. Even in this era."

Once inside, she took the baby from Henry and, after a quick snuggle and a peck on the baby's cheek, she handed him to a woman who appeared to be waiting to take charge. Carrying the young prince with care, she made her way up the grand staircase.

"Don't worry. That is my trusted confidante, Lady Mary Catherine. You can trust her." Marie de Guise motioned to the room on the right. "Shall we? Lady Mary Catherine will join us once the young prince is fed, changed and settled into his new rooms."

"What do you call this place?" Henry asked as he followed his ancestors into what appeared to be some sort of common room.

"This room is called the living room," Mary Elizabeth chose to answer, entering the room behind her grandmother and the Scottish king. "The building is called a house. Though some people might refer to it as a mansion because of its large size."

"You call this large?" Henry's eyebrows arched upwards.

"Well, perhaps not in the standard we're used to," Mary Elizabeth chuckled softly. "It's certainly not a castle."

"But it is home," Marie de Guise added. "And there's the famous quote, 'My home is like a castle'."

"I think you might be referring to an old English law," Henry shook his head, marvelling at the idea this house, as Mary Elizabeth called it, might be considered a castle. "The English lawyer and politician, Sir Edward Coke, established this as a common law in 1628, I believe. Something along the lines of: 'For a man's house is his castle, et domus sua cuique est tutissimum refugium'."

"And each man's home is his safest refuge," Mary Elizabeth translated the Latin. "You know your history well. My nephew, King Charles I of England, did one thing right in allowing Sir Edward to establish the law. It doesn't mean much. But the sentiment rings true."

Henry paced the room, admiring the fine woodwork on the mantle over the fireplace and the portrait of Mary Elizabeth as a princess above it. "You make a beautiful princess, Grandmother. And you will be a beautiful queen." He addressed his many times removed great grandmother with fondness. "And you were," turning to wink, "and still are a beautiful woman." He wasn't sure at what point in his ancestor's life he had appeared. However, he suspected it was sometime during Mary Elizabeth's retreat at Kirkwall Castle in the Orkney's awaiting the death of Queen Elizabeth I and the accession of her brother to the throne of England.

Mary Elizabeth blushed. "Thank you, young man. You make

a handsome king yourself. And a good one, too."

"Enough pleasantries, children," Marie de Guise scolded lightly. *"We have much to discuss."*

They all nodded in agreement.

Henry spoke first, however. And rather unexpectedly. "I need to know. Is the young prince mine?" Henry was blunt and to the point. Even he didn't know where the idea originated. "I love him as if he were mine, but with all my wife's dalliances, I do wonder. I believe there is a way to test this in the twenty-fifth century?"

"Yes," Marie de Guise nodded. *"DNA testing."*

"What's DNA testing?" Henry scrunched his eyebrows in concentration, choosing to take a seat so he could listen more intently.

"Genealogy is the study of one's ancestry," Marie de Guise began. *"It became a popular hobby for many people in the late twentieth- and early twenty-first centuries. People wanted to know the extent of their family trees. Simply put, DNA is studying the gene-makeup of an individual and comparing it with possible matches. Everyone has genes; it's part of our biological makeup. There are other methods of testing, like the ABO blood group typing, but DNA is considered the most reliable method of testing parentage. Paternity DNA testing is practiced in cases where men want reassurance the baby the woman carried was in fact theirs. As in your case. Basically, there is no half-way margin in the test results. If the probability of parentage is 0%, then the parent is not biologically related to the child. If the probability of parentage is 99.99%, then the parent is biologically related to the child."*

Henry sat, staring at his great ancestor. He found it amazing a woman who lived hundreds of years before him could grasp some of the most scientific developments almost a hundred years after his recorded passing. He shook his head as if to clear the cobwebs in his brain. "Amazing. Confusing, complicated, but amazing nevertheless." He sat quietly a bit longer. "So how do we go about this, what did you call it? Oh yes, DNA testing?"

"Quite simply. I need to take a swab from your cheek."

"A what?" he gasped, eyes bulging in surprise.

"This test is done by collecting what is known as buccal cells," Marie de Guise explained carefully. "These cells are found inside a person's cheek. The cells are collected using a cheek swab with a wooden or plastic stick handle. The cotton collector tip of the swab is rubbed on the inside of the cheek. We would need to collect buccal cells from both you and your son, to compare the match."

Henry was flummoxed and the expression on his face showed it. "And how do you know all this?"

"I read a lot." A safe enough answer. "I just so happen to have a kit in my study. I had expected your visit and anticipated your request."

"You did?"

"I did." The woman had a warm, sweet smile that she displayed as if pacifying a child. "I quite understand your concerns, Henry. This is the right thing to do. But even without the test, I can assure you the child is yours in every way it matters."

"And you know this, how?"

Her smile continued its intent to act as a pacifier. "Never mind, how. I just do. Now we shall do this test and send it off to a trusted lab for testing."

"And how long does it take?"

"A few weeks. You should pop back to visit your son in a few weeks' time. We'll have the results by then." She left the room to retrieve the DNA kit.

Mary Elizabeth had been sitting quietly on the couch all this time. She finally spoke, "I feel like a fly on the wall." And she giggled.

"What a wonderful idea," Henry replied. "Perhaps I should use your ruse to spy on my enemies. Or, at least to find out who my enemies are."

"It's not a safe life being royal," Mary Elizabeth noted. "I have done it, lived the life of a royal spy, many times. Although, I really wasn't a fly. I just managed to remain hidden in the shadows so I could listen and observe."

"Good strategy. I should make use of this time travel skill to my advantage."

"Yes, you should."

They were interrupted when Marie de Guise returned, Lady Mary Catherine just behind her. "He's settling into his new nursery nicely. He's been fed, changed and now he sleeps."

"It's amazing how much this place is like the one I grew up in," Mary Elizabeth commented.

"I had this house reconstructed after it was destroyed, with a few modifications based on lessons learned. And it has remained a safe haven ever since." Marie de Guise had built a marvellous mansion, on the same site as the previous twenty-first century house, the one which exploded after the ladies made a last-minute exit to the past to avoid danger which was threatening them in the future. All terribly confusing. Even he had difficulty wrapping his mind around this time traveling gig. Past, present, future, time was ethereal, illusive, and not always what you hoped or expected. "Now. Let's swab your cheek." Marie de Guise held up the cotton tipped swab. "But do remember this testing is not conclusive. Should your son be the child of anyone in the Stuart dynasty, a definitive association to your DNA may not be possible."

"Understood." Henry nodded. At least, he thought he understood. But who else in the Stuart clan could possibly be the father? Bertie? The thought was there and gone in less than a flash.

NINETEEN

Holyrood House, Edinburgh, Sometime in the Future

"He knows too much." A deep-toned voice, possibly a man's voice, echoed in the distance. "And now there's another body needing an implant."

"You mean the one he claims to be his son. Prince Edward." This voice, high pitched, definitely female. What did she mean by 'claimed to be'? Edward was his son. Wasn't he?

"Yes. Otherwise the young prince will be stuck forever in the twenty-first century. He has a role to play in the nineteenth-century. He has to be capable of moving through time. Only infants can escape through the portals of time without an implant."

"He's stirring. I hear a moan. Do you think he heard us?"

"Can't be sure. Might be an idea to give him another blocker to erase the memories of what he may or may not have heard."

"Where am I?" Henry groaned. "What is this place?"

"You are perfectly safe, here, Your Majesty." The woman's voice came closer until his foggy vision cleared enough so he could see her standing over him. "You are in Holyrood House, Your Majesty. Just resting from a recent surgery."

"Surgery. What surgery?" A prick in the arm. Blackness overtook him. Again.

TWENTY

The Cave, Scotland Wilds, Autumn, Year of Our Lord 1875

Henry woke to the chill and the aches which accompanied the discomfort of sleeping on a cold, hard packed, dirt floor. The embers in the fire had long since died out. The rain outside abated.

He studied the men lying around the cave and the one half asleep at the entrance, presumably standing guard. James was nowhere to be seen. Henry hadn't expected to see James again. Not here. Not now.

Hearing the king moving about, the others made attempts to awaken as well. It was time to make haste to Edinburgh. Henry knew his son was safe. But for how long? The others with him in the cave knew nothing of what had transpired at Holyrood House. Or did they? Was there a spy even amongst his most trusted guards here in the cave?

"Saddle up," he ordered as he pushed himself off the ground, picking up the cape he had wrapped around him for meagre warmth during the night. He gave it a good shake before tossing it across his shoulders. It was damp, but if the sun was managing to peak through the thick overgrowth cloaking the hillside, the cape, and himself, would dry quickly and provide him with some comfort on the ride. "We must go. Now." There was no time to bank up the fire. No time for a morning repast. They had to make haste.

"Yes, Your Majesty," came a chorus of grunts and accolades. The men were honorable, trustworthy. Henry only had the best close by. Robbie had helped him select the men. He trusted Robbie and Robbie trusted these men. He hoped his trust wasn't misplaced. He had to trust someone.

They saddled, mounted and made their way across the hillock and down the other side, only to mount another hillock after circumnavigating the valley and the rushing stream which ran through its center. They maintained this course most of the morning, up and down, splashing through streams and keeping their mounts at a steady pace. They didn't stop to eat or drink, only a little water for the horses before they crossed the last stream before entering the outskirts of Edinburgh.

They made their way directly to Holyrood House. They entered the main courtyard and dismounted, handing the horses' leads to the stable boys who came rushing out. "Give them a good rubdown, lads," Henry called out as he dashed towards the main entrance. "And an extra serving of oats. They deserve it."

"Yes, Your Majesty," was echoed several times as the boys acknowledged his orders before going about the task.

Henry entered the main hall and was greeted by a rather disturbed guard. "Your Majesty. Something terrible has happened." The guard all but sputtered, shifting from one foot to another. "Someone must have spiked our food or drink. We were only knocked out for about an hour. Long enough for them to take your son."

"Them? Who?" Henry's voice struggled to maintain calm. He was angry, but hopefully he could rely on the fact his son was safe. He came here first in the hopes of ascertaining the guilty persons. He knew the nanny was part of the plot, but who was the Englishman in the nursery, the extremely angry Englishman?

He didn't wait for an answer. He knew there wouldn't be one. The guards didn't know any more than he did. Tossing his muddied cape along with his gloves on a nearby chair, Henry dashed up the main staircase, taking two steps at a time as he left a trail of mud in his wake. He stormed into the nursery to find his son's attendants in a fluster, not knowing what to do or who to blame.

"What happened? Where's Miss Margaret? Bring her to me now!"

The ladies studied each other. No one wanted to speak. Finally, the woman who served as the young prince's nursemaid stepped forward. She curtseyed, rather awkwardly, then started to speak. "She's..." she stumbled, not sure how to continue. "We found her..." Breaking into shudders of sobs, she merely pointed in the direction of the room where the baby slept.

Henry rushed into the room. It was in shambles. The walls were split open, kicked or crushed by a sharp object. The corner which hid the secret staircase was still intact more or less, his secret secure for now. The cradle was overturned and the baby items scattered helter-skelter across the floor. In the center of all this mess lay the body of Edward's nanny. He didn't need to look any closer to realize she was dead. The amount of blood caking the back of her neck and pooling around her upper body attested to the fact. So much for learning anything from her.

He returned to the main room of the nursery. Looking at each woman astutely, studying them closely, he demanded, "Where's my son?" No one answered. "What happened here? Who did this?"

"We fell asleep, Your Majesty," the nursemaid whimpered.

"The guards who woke us said everyone was drugged. Miss Margaret was already dead," she fidgeted nervously at the word, 'dead', "and the young prince gone."

"Who was here before this happened?"

"An English lord, Your Majesty. He claimed he was here to see you and he would await your return. But he's no longer here."

"What English lord?"

"Perhaps I can answer your question." It was the voice of the guard he had met in the main hall. "Lord Dudley of the Lake District. Very abrasive. Didn't trust him. Set guards to watch him, but I guess he got the better of us all."

"How long ago?"

"Just hours."

"Go after him. He can't have gone far. You know the land between here and the border better than anyone. You've also seen this man and will recognize him. Get him. Bring him back."

"Yes, Your Majesty." The guard bowed smartly and left to do the king's bidding.

"Have someone remove the body. Then you ladies must clean up the mess."

"Yes, Your Majesty." The women chorused, somewhat unsure of the situation, yet relieved to have been issued orders they could follow.

Henry made an abrupt turn on his heel and stormed out of the room, his anger barely contained. How dare anyone threaten his family!

He made his way to his chambers where his attendant was waiting to help him clean up and put on fresh, dry clothes. The shivers subsided once he had changed. He dismissed his man, locked the doors and made way for the secret panel leading to the same staircase. He squeezed inside, pulling the panel securely shut behind him. He went up, instead of down. Mary Elizabeth was right. It was time he started spying on all those around him. He wanted to listen in on the conversations while the nursery was being tidied. Someone knew something and neither he, nor his son, was safe in this building until he knew who was involved in the conspiracy.

Settled inside the hidden space near his son's nursery, Henry listened intently. "You have to tell him." It was Robbie.

"I can't, my lord." A woman's voice. One of the nursery attendants, but which one, he couldn't be sure.

"He needs to know." Footsteps thundered away, the only sounds left were the sniffles of women as they set about cleaning the nursery.

"Your Majesty." It was Robbie. Down below. Just outside his own chambers.

Henry made his way back down the stairs and entered his chambers, carefully closing the panel shut behind him. Robbie sounded frantic. "Your Majesty. You must escape. I must see you safely away from here. Before..." His next words were cut off as the door crashed open and his man's limp body was thrust inwards.

"How dare you!" Henry greeted the hulk of man invading his private space.

"I dare on the commands of my queen, Victoria, Queen of England. And soon to be Queen of Scotland as well."

"I don't think so." Henry maintained his calm with a demure smile. "And you are?"

"Arthur Dudley, Lord Warden of the Marches. You needn't have sent your man to bring me back. I have my orders and I wouldn't dream of leaving Edinburgh until I had followed all of my orders." He paused briefly, allowing his words to hang in the air long enough to garner some sort of reaction from the Scottish king. Not satisfied, the lord decided to poke deeper. "I am here on behalf of Her Majesty, Queen Victoria, who will one day rule all of Scotland as well as England. After I remove you and your son and take your wife home to the English court, the English will invade and the Scottish crown will be no more. It's what should have happened hundreds of years ago. If it hadn't been for your Stuart ancestor, Queen Mary Elizabeth, you would not exist and neither would your crown. Now. Where is the young prince? You have obviously spirited him away somewhere you deem safe."

"I have, but you'll never find him."

"Don't be so sure. Guards." The irksome English lord bellowed. He glanced away from Henry for mere seconds. But it was long enough. Henry made a quick decision. It was time to move out of this time. To the future. But how far? At what point could he fix this problem? Or could he fix this problem? It was time to visit his once favorite cousin, Bertie, the Prince of Wales. But when? And where? There had been a time when they were friends, trusted confidantes. Were they still? Now was the time to test the waters, so to speak.

The Lord of the Marches returned his gaze to the king. Or, at least where the king had once stood.

"Find him!" he bellowed.

TWENTY-ONE

HMSS Serapis, Enroute to India, October, Year of Our Lord 1875

"It's a fine ship, the Serapis," Henry leaned over the rail, standing next to his cousin as they both feasted their eyes on the calm blue waters. It wasn't always like this. A gentle rock of the ship as waves splashed lazily against her hull. The ocean could be a fierce companion. Today, however, it was calm. "A fine day to take in the fresh sea air."

"Henry," Bertie boomed with his usual exuberance, letting out a puff of his cigar, allowing the smoke to drift across the open water, before turning to greet the Scottish king. "I didn't know you were on board. Oh! Wait! No! You jumped through time again, didn't you?" Bertie was one of the few non-time travelers who knew about Henry's ability to jump through time, a secret he swore to keep. However, it was a secret he kept reluctantly, almost jealous since he couldn't do what Henry could do. What a blast it must be to jump through time. Bertie would use the talent to jump from one bordello to another! All over the world. He had managed to keep the secret. It was more out of self preservation. Who would believe him, anyway? Time travel? Not a chance.

They'd all think he was daft and there were plenty of people who already believed he was.

Henry continued to scan the waters. He decided it was best to let Bertie take the lead in the conversation. "So, what can I do for you now?" the English prince finally asked, barely masking the tone of exasperation in his voice. "You know I'm half a world away from Mother, so I can't intervene on your behalf. She wouldn't listen anyway. The captain says we'll be at our destination in a few days. India. Who would have thought she'd allow her heir to venture so far from her powerful grasp?"

"India. One of the many countries under the cruel English controlling fist of power."

"Now Henry. You're putting it a bit harsh, don't you think?" Bertie argued, taking another draw from his cigar and slowly exhaling the smoke which slithered away in the gentle breeze washing across the waters and the upper deck where the men stood. "We're not all bad, you know."

"And yet the English crown still wants to control Scotland and all its colonies." Henry pivoted so he was only half leaning on the rail. He wanted to study Bertie's face as he grilled him, challenged him. "You know your mother sent someone to kidnap my son, so he could be brought up in the English royal court and married off to one of your daughters. The same person your mother sent was intent on taking my life as well. Now how do you explain it?" He couldn't resist the urge to point his finger into Bertie's chest, something he had often done in his younger years, something his cousin didn't like one bit.

Bertie let out a cough, as if he were choking on his cigar. A stickler for his appearance, it was a wonder he favored this appalling vice. Dressed, meticulously as always, in a tweed outfit, sporting a Homburg hat and Norfolk jacket and trouser legs pressed from side to side, a personal preference and a style he promoted, Bertie had the look of both casual comfortable and formally important. He was obviously a man who was never uncomfortable with who he was or how he appeared to others. "My dear fellow. I have no idea what you're talking about. But the charade you led back in the spring, evicting us, the English royals from Scotland, and convicting your wife to a life imprisoned in a ghastly medieval castle where none other than our ancestor, Mary Queen of Scots, was imprisoned. It was all a bit much. Having Mother, and myself as well, escorted to the border and forbidden admittance ever again to Scotland. You did go a bit far. Turned the hand, so to speak." He paused to take another puff of his cigar. Leaving it between his teeth, he half muttered, "You do realize they're going to name Mother, Empress of India. It's the whole reason for my trip here. To boost morale and promote her influence, her importance, and her imperial power."

Henry snorted. "Right. Through abuse and bully tactics."

"Now, Henry." The prince shook his head. "Don't be so harsh. You've been known to use bully tactics on occasion. Your wife being the most recent example."

"I have never and will never bully anyone, let alone my wife." He could almost taste the venom of his words, but he didn't stop his tyrannical words of self defense. "I had to protect what is mine, Bertie." Henry was barely able to control the mounting anger. He knew his cousin could be a bit pompous at times, but pointing an accusing finger at him? Too much. "Scotland is mine and my son's. Not England's. And it never will be. My wife and your mother have been threatening me and what's mine for some time now."

"So, you claim," Bertie snapped back, his anger equally evident in his barely contained expression. "She would never have married your son to one of my daughters, you know. Too closely related and all."

"And what do you mean by that?" Henry moved closer to his cousin, seeking restitution and a plausible explanation. "Are you

suggesting Edward is not mine? Perhaps yours?" The thought had never entered his mind before this, but it was entirely possible. Isabel had grown up in the English court and Bertie had easy access to her. He was the flamboyant ladies' man after all.

"Time will reveal all." Avoiding further direct confrontation, Bertie returned his concentration to the waters below, his usual stance to prevent others from witnessing his distress. "So, who did she send?"

"Arthur Dudley."

Bertie guffawed, which converted into another fit of coughing. When he recovered, he said, "Never did fully recover from the bout of typhoid a few years back. A real miracle I survived at all. I do hope this dry air in India helps."

"They have typhoid epidemics too, Bertie. And I'm sure your smoking doesn't help." He couldn't avoid the lecture tone of voice.

"Yes, they do. And my smoking soothes, not hinders my condition." He cleared his throat. "So, she sent the Lord Warden of the Marches. A real brute of a man." He shook his head. "We'd be better off without men like him. He takes an order and manipulates it in such a way no one benefits and the end result is a lot of casualties." He patted his cousin fondly on the shoulder closest to him. "I am sorry, my dear old fellow. But there is nothing I can do for you. Except offer my sympathies and perhaps have a chat, face to face, with my dear mother. When I do get to see her again. Which, of course, won't be for another year or two."

"Bertie." A woman's voice, perhaps his wife, perhaps his latest mistress, called from behind the men. "Who are you talking to?"

Bertie was about to explain when he noticed his cousin had vanished.

TWENTY-TWO

Stirling Castle, Late Fall, Year of Our Lord 1875

Henry loved this old castle. He had spent considerable time and money on multiple renovations to keep the castle liveable as well as fortified to face whatever late nineteenth century warfare could throw its way. Scottish royal history was invincibly connected with this powerful stronghold. Situated on the peak of an intrusive crag, known as Castle Hill, in the tiny community of Stirling, the castle had a reputation of being almost impenetrable from invading forces. It was surrounded on three sides by steep cliffs, giving it a strategic advantage of a strong defensive position. With thick, stone walled ramparts, the sprawling castle, much of which dated from the fourteenth and fifteenth centuries (though some of it was built much earlier), was the birthplace of countless Scottish kings and queens, many of whom had also married at Stirling and held court in the castle. It was a good place to hide out, which was Henry's intent. At least until the English assassins seeking his untimely death were caught and dealt with.

He had managed to slip through the iron grasp of the Lord of the Marches. Initially playing along with his capture, Henry had secured some valuable intel. Queen Victoria's instructions had been to bring both the Scottish king and his heir to the royal court at Windsor. Lord Dudley had only managed to secure Henry as his prisoner for a few minutes at most. He had tried to grill the king, to no avail. Even if Henry had told him the prince's whereabouts, Lord Dudley wouldn't have believed him.

The Lord of the Marches had an explosive temper. Barely contained. Henry knew he had no alternative than to just vanish into the time warp. It was the only way. Who knew what this temper-infested man would do when he thoroughly unleashed his fury on the king? The quick decision to leap through time had been executed with precision. After his quick jump to visit his cousin, Henry returned to his time. Though not to Holyrood House. He returned to Stirling Castle.

Reports from Edinburgh outlined the destructive nature of Lord Dudley's search for Henry, not just in Holyrood House, but in the entire city. Anyone standing in his way was executed on the spot. Bodies, bloodied and lifeless, littered the streets and the halls of the great homes, including his own.

What have I done to deserve this? Henry repeated this question like a mantra, over and over again in his head, as he slept, as he paced the ramparts, the battlements and the courtyard, and as he wandered from room to room. *What have I done to deserve this? What have I done to deserve this? What have I done to deserve this?*

The past few weeks had been spent sheltered in the castle, just wandering here and there. He barely communicated with the others, not wanting to allow his people to see how anomalous his situation was. Things were precarious at best, insecure almost to the point of obscurity. He couldn't allow people to see his lack of faith, such as it was. He felt extremely insecure and didn't quite know which way to turn and what to do to ease the current volatile environment surrounding him and threatening his people.

He was bereft in grief over the unnecessary loss of both men and women. The loss of his trusted men through deceit and death lay heavy on his heart and mind. The loss of a trusted marital partner at his side rankled him.

Exhausted from restless sleep and lack thereof, Henry resorted to pacing, looking beyond the castle ramparts, studying military strategies, and thinking. He was deep in thought when the pounding on the door to his outer chambers alerted him.

"Your Majesty." It was Robbie. Henry couldn't believe it. He thought Robbie had been killed at the hands of the vicious bully English lord.

"Robbie?" he called out and rushed to let him in. "You're alive. I thought..." He grabbed the man in a big bear hug, patting him fondly on the back.

Robbie flinched from a mixture of pain and embarrassment. He wasn't accustomed to bear hugs from the king and he had sustained injuries which still bothered him. "Not quite. Still alive. I was out for some time. One of the housemaids rescued me and hid me in her chambers. Nursed me back to health. Lovely girl." He blushed and cleared his throat. "And here we are. I gather he did a number on you as well."

Henry waved the concerns away. "No. I managed to escape before he could show himself to be the brute he is. Glad to be away from him. Glad you are, too." He motioned his man into the room and shut the door behind him, locking it to ensure privacy.

"Not for long, I fear." Robbie walked with a slight limp, evidence he was still in the process of healing from his injuries. He made his way to the fireplace and took a seat. "I hope you don't mind."

Henry shook his head. "I don't stand on ceremony in here,

Robbie. You know better than anyone. So, what do you mean, not for long?"

"He's been prowling the countryside looking for you," Robbie replied. "He's learned of your whereabouts and he's on his way to Stirling as we speak."

"He's not one to give up easily, is he? Well, we know Stirling's history. He'll have a hard time laying siege on this castle. It's why I came here. I've sent out a call to my most trusted chieftains. They should be here within the day. We'll plan our line of defense. Lord Dudley will soon rue the day he was sent to conquer Scotland. I fear we shall have to put an end to him, to wipe the scourge of his presence from our fair land and to send a message to the English queen: Scotland is not to be trifled with."

"True enough."

Yelling came from below. Footsteps clattered quickly towards Henry's chambers from the hall beyond his door. A knock. "Your Majesty," a voice called from the other side of the door. Henry made no move to unlock it. "The MacGregor has arrived and is waiting in the grand hall."

"Tell him I'll be right down," Henry called back. The footsteps retreated. "And the planning begins, Robbie. Let's go meet the MacGregor. The Murrays should be arriving next. And hopefully the Ogilvies will be close behind. We shall have a force to be reckoned with."

"Perhaps with our well garrisoned fortress here, well armed, and troops waiting in the woods beyond, we can surround the English bastard," Robbie suggested. "Then we might have a chance."

"My thoughts exactly. Let's go talk to the MacGregor chief."

Moments later, the two men marched into the grand hall. "Ian my friend," Henry spoke with fondness for his childhood friend. "Thank you for coming." He nodded briskly to the other

MacGregors scattered around the room before returning his focus to Ian. Decked in the MacGregor plaid kilt, its bright reds and greens making a startling contrast against the meagre lines of black, the robust man made a commanding appearance. A wide belt encircled his waist and the finely crafted dirk perched from its sheath at his side. His thick auburn hair, long, curly and unruly, lay carelessly around his ruddy face. Thickset and solid, he was the craven image of a strong Highland warrior. He was also one of the king's closest friends. An honor he obviously didn't take lightly.

"Your Majesty. No thanks needed." Ian MacGregor, clan chief, wrapped his thick hand around his king, exchanging warm greetings, patting each other's shoulders. "The English scourge is upon us again. We must band together and erase the problem."

"Well. At least remove it from our realm," Henry politely corrected.

"Exactly."

Henry motioned for Ian to sit. They chose facing chairs beside the hearth with its blazing fire. The other MacGregors stood and sat in various locations around the large room.

"Anything you can tell me? What's happening beyond these walls?" Henry asked a stream of questions. "Tell me what you know. And does this have anything to do with the nefarious activities you reported to me earlier?"

"Well, you probably know as much as I do, Your Majesty." He nodded at Robbie. "I'm sure your man has brought you up-to-date on the happenings between here and Edinburgh."

Henry nodded. "He has."

"And I do believe we have an escalation of earlier activities to ignite violence within our realm," Ian continued by answering the last question. "Only now the attack is being more direct. Targeted at you and your son." He glanced around. "He is safe, isn't he? Here?"

"He's safe," Henry answered. "But not here. So, how do we proceed?"

"I assume the others have been called."

"Aye." Henry used the Scottish colloquialism to respond. He only spoke casually when with close friends and confidantes. Ian was both. They had grown up together. For many of his younger years, Henry had spent considerable time at Glenlyon Castle in Perthshire, home of the MacGregor chiefs. They had shared mock battles on the grounds surrounding the castle and studied together in the schoolroom on the top floor. When the boys weren't at Glenlyon, they were at Stirling, or Holyrood House, or Blair Castle, also in Perthshire, home of the Murray chiefs, or Airlie Castle in Angus, home of the Ogilvie chiefs. All of these buildings had a lot of history full of intrigue. As boys, they learned the secret passageways of each dwelling and lived with a passion for excitement and adventure.

The others Ian was referring to included Bruce Murray and Wallace Ogilvie who had also spent some of their boyhood years with the young prince who became their king. They had formed a strong bond, full of loyalty. Henry could always depend on the MacGregors, the Murrays and the Ogilvies to come to his aid. There were other clans he trusted, but these he held closest to his heart.

"They should be here within a day," Henry continued. "In the meantime, we can start planning our strategy. This Lord Dudley is about as mean as they come. And, I'm sure he's quite the strategist. But we have the advantage. He doesn't know Scotland and he certainly doesn't know Stirling Castle."

"He may know more than you think." Ian stretched out his legs, making himself comfortable. "He spent some years in Scotland when he was a lad. His mother's lineage traces back to the Clan Sinclair."

"Really? From way up north?" Henry shook his head in disbelief. "Then he'll know this land better than we would hope."

"Aye. But I don't believe he's ever been to Stirling. And, even if he had been here, he wouldn't know the castle as we do. Certainly not with all the renovations and improvements you've made over the years."

"True enough." Henry was bolstered by his friend's note of confidence. The men sat in companionable silence for a few minutes, the only sounds permeating their space coming from the fire in the hearth and the MacGregor men shuffling and coughing discreetly. Henry copied his friend, stretching his legs out comfortably in front of him, allowing the warmth from the flames to creep up his legs and engulf the rest of his body.

"He's a military man," Ian broke the silence. "Trained with an English regiment in India, I believe. He'll know how to fight, how to lay a siege."

"As only the English can do." Henry shuffled restlessly. He never was one who could sit still for long. "Properly formatted lines of defense, all attacks done with military precision and the need to show one's presence and one's prowess."

"All show and little logic. It's how the English lost the American colonies. And it's how Lord Dudley will lose yet another battle with Scotland. We don't fight by English rules of battle. We fight to persevere. We fight to win."

"Amen to that." Henry nodded in agreement.

TWENTY-THREE

Malmohus Castle, Denmark, April, Year of Our Lord 1577

"Ah! Another Scottish king. And you are?" The dusty heap of blankets was tossed aside and a scarred, emaciated figure of a man pushed himself into a sitting position on the rickety cot on which he had been, presumably, sleeping.

"King Henry, my Lord Bothwell."

"James. Call me James. I am no longer lord of anything." The man cleared his throat. "This retched place will be the death of me. So, what era do you call your own?"

"The late 1800s."

James raised an eyebrow which was marked by a slash just barely healing. How could anything heal in this dank place? In this filth? Henry doubted the man had been allowed clean water to bathe. At least, not recently. "And what brings you back in time to see the likes of me?"

"You are my ancestor. You were also a great battle commander. I come seeking advice on how to defeat the English once and for all."

The decrepit figure tried to laugh, but it quickly transformed into a fit of coughing. When the fit subsided, he gave the young king an intense look. "You can't defeat the English, lad. We've tried for centuries, long before I was born. All you can do is try to keep them at bay."

"You've fought enough battles with the English to be able to spare me some words of advice, James." Henry was not about to give up. Lord Bothwell had been an astute battle commander in his day. Long before he was imprisoned for kidnapping Mary Queen of Scots and forcing her to marry him. At least, it's the way the opposing political powers of the day painted the picture. Mary Elizabeth was his daughter and she told a completely different story about counterespionage which would make the spies as far forward in time as the twenty-first century and perhaps even beyond look like amateurs.

"Aye. Marie de Guise suggested you might come to me for advice. It's all I can give you, lad. Advice. Don't fight on principal. Fight to win at all cost. The best defence is the offence. A good offence. You start the battle. Don't wait for the English to strike first. They're trespassing, if I'm understanding correctly." Henry nodded in response. "Then you have every right to ambush them and take them prisoner. And, if you have this wonderful ability to jump through time, as Marie de Guise and my daughter, Mary Elizabeth, do, then make a visit to the English monarch and put the fear of the Scottish clans in his or her heart. He or she'll think twice before trying to invade Scotland a second time."

"She. Queen Victoria." Henry took a minute to explain. "She's a power force of her own. She rules a good portion of the world and dares to call herself Empress of the English Empire overseas. Scotland rules a greater portion of the world. Kindlier and more civil than the English, I might add. She wants what we have. She wants it all."

"Don't they all." Bothwell didn't try to mask the sarcasm in his voice. "Every English monarch in history has wanted a piece of what we have. And more, too." He paused to endure another fit of coughing. When it subsided, he continued, "I gather from Mary Elizabeth's visits you have further developed what she initiated during her reign. Universal education. Advanced research in science, mathematics and medicine. Promoting and supporting the arts. Humanitarian aid to struggling populations around the world. Given these accomplishments, I would say you are more of a power to reckon with than this Queen Victoria."

"Perhaps. So, you suggest we surround the invaders and take advantage of a surprise attack."

"Before they have an opportunity to catch onto your tactics."

"In other words, before it's too late."

"Aye. And allow no escapes. All the invaders must be either killed or imprisoned. Don't allow them to return to England as they'll just be back. They'll know your tactics the next time they come and they'll be better prepared."

"Good advice."

"I believe you have some penal colonies scattered around the world. Or, so I hear from my daughter. Send the prisoners there. The further away and more isolated the outpost, the better."

"Way up north. An isolated island encased in snow and ice. Only the Eskimos roam free on Baffin Island. I'll send them there. They won't be able to escape unless they want to tempt the fates of the cold, desolate, barren land and waters plagued with icebergs."

"Perfect. What do you call this land?"

"Northern Nova Scotia."

"New Scotland."

"Grandmother. It's what I call your daughter. She claims an alternate timeline, one quite different from the one we know, a timeline that existed before she changed the course of history, creating this vast continent known as Canada. Even as far north as Baffin Island. I prefer to keep the name, Nova Scotia."

"*Very fitting for a grand new land for the Scottish Empire.*"

"*Encased in ice, these prisoners will never escape.*" Henry felt confident in his decisions. It felt good talking to this ancestor. Reassuring. Stimulating. He noticed James was perking up as well. Imprisoned in a Danish prison for the crime of loving and marrying a queen. Didn't seem right. Here he was languishing away in this rotten hole. For a moment in his time, his life brightened as he played a vital role in the strategic planning of a military exercise well beyond his future.

"*Surround and conquer.*" James studied the king before him, reassured one of his descendants had managed to retain the Scottish fervor centuries beyond his lifetime.

"*Surround and conquer.*" Henry echoed the older man's sentiments. "*For now and forever.*"

"*Aye. For now and forever.*"

TWENTY-FOUR

Osborne House, Isle of Wight, English Channel, Late Fall, Year of Our Lord 1875

Victoria had inhabited this grand palatial home in the winter months since her late husband, Prince Albert, had designed and built it in the 1840s. Styled after an Italian Renaissance palazzo, the house was more of a castle than a meagre dwelling. She liked it here.

The building rambled, both inside and out and Queen Victoria enjoyed rambling through its rooms. It was a restless pastime helping her come to terms with the current issues plaguing her mind. Scotland was top of the list this time. News from her English spies in Scotland was not good. King Henry had managed to uncover her plot, rescue his son and sequestered him somewhere intensely secret. She needed to know. She needed the prince. He was the future of a combined, amalgamated Great Britain. Yes, she would call it Great Britain. Even if the prince was actually her grandson instead of a distant cousin. The world didn't need to know the details. The world only knew what she, queen, empress, ruler of the world (her ultimate goal), allowed the world to know.

Once she secured the Scottish empire as her own, she would rename the blasted piece of her continent, the northern lands of the new world, lands of what should rightfully be hers, lands which had plagued her ancestors since they'd been discovered and settled. King George III had to lose a good piece of the new continent to what was now called the United States of America. They had never managed to get a foothold north of the St. Lawrence River. The Scottish and the French controlled it. More the Scottish now, as the French became too embroiled in their own battles on home soil to have the resources to maintain the colony. If her memories served her right, it was shortly after her coronation when Scotland actually purchased from France the French colonies along the St. Lawrence River. Scotland seldom went to battle. Only when threatened on their own turf. She was threatening them now. Would they have the military force to fight back? Would they have the military strategy to succeed?

"I wonder." *She was deep in thought as she made her way into the library, happy to notice the fire roaring in the hearth, keeping the room toasty warm. There was a smile on her face, a smile of contentment, as if all was well in her world or, at least, soon would be.*

"You wonder what?" *The voice, a man's, startled her. She hadn't realized she was talking out loud. To herself. It would never do. She didn't need any help spreading rumors suggesting their ruling monarch talked to herself. Her hand jumped to her chest to sooth the rapid beating of her heart.*

"Who goes there?"

"Your cousin. The one you plan to exterminate." *Henry stepped out of the shadows at the end of a large bookcase.*

"Henry. What are you doing here? How did you get here?" *She moved towards the fireplace and was about to reach out to tug the bell pull, to call someone, anyone, to her defense. Henry grabbed her hand before she could reach the bell pull. She jumped back a step, pulling her hand from his grasp, affronted at the brash move. How dare anyone touch her! Prevent her from what she deemed her right to do. She wasn't sure how to respond, suddenly feeling rather skittish. It was inconceivable for Henry to simply pop in. The last she heard, he was somewhere in the heart of his own realm, far in the north. He couldn't possibly ride this far south, hop a ferry and be here to visit with her without her prior knowledge. With her network of spies, nothing escaped her noticed. Or did it?*

"I wouldn't." He stood with arms crossed in front of him, positioning himself between her and the bell pull, preventing her from trying again to summon help. "We need to talk, Cousin. You need to call off your men. You won't rescue my wife, for however long she remains my wife. You won't kidnap my son and you definitely won't pawn him off to one of your female minions." He watched his cousin, frozen, her arm still reaching as if to tug the bell pull, which he blocked. "I think you should sit, Cousin, and explain to me why you are making this into a war. Because that's what it is. You continue along this path, and I will declare war on England. You may not like the results of doing battle with the Scots."

Victoria let her hand drop and stepped back to sit in her favorite reading chair. It held no comfort for her as she fumed inside with the knowledge her cousin, the King of Scotland, knew more of her plans than she would have liked.

"It sounds like you're threatening me, Henry. It's never a good idea to threaten a neighboring ruling monarch."

"And yet you feel obliged to threaten me, Cousin? I am your neighboring ruling monarch, am I not?" He worded it more like statements than questions. "Having my wife spy on me, plot against me. Your son pretending to befriend me. Sending one your English minions to kidnap my son. Which, I might add, he was unsuccessful in his attempt. He was also unsuccessful in

assassinating me. Tomorrow, he will be in captivity. Mine. Either that or dead."

Victoria shuddered, struggling to maintain her composure. "It's all part of the art of diplomacy, Henry. Something you, of all people, should know."

"It's all part of your grand scheme to make what is mine, yours. Greed. That's what it is. And you always were a greedy ..." He didn't finish his thoughts, biting his upper lip to prevent further insults from escaping his mouth.

"Think what you will, Henry. Now, if you're done with the insults, I think I'll order up some tea. Would you care for some?" She took her eyes off the Scottish king just long enough to reach another bell pull, one secretly handy to her chair. When she returned her gaze to the place where he had been towering over her, he was gone.

TWENTY-FIVE

Stirling Castle, Late Fall, Year of Our Lord 1875

His cousin's words rang in his ears. "The art of diplomacy," she had said. Her definition of diplomacy certainly wasn't his. He always believed diplomacy executed a significant margin of caring, of compassion. Perhaps he was an anomaly, an exception to the rule. If there was a rule.

Then there was his great ancestor, Lord Bothwell. His advice wasn't much, but it was important. "Surround and conquer," he had said. He claimed it was the best way to defeat an invading English army. He would certainly try.

"Your Majesty. The Murray scout has managed to break through the English lines without detection. He's here." Robbie marched smartly into the grand hall where the MacGregors continued to lounge while their chief talked to the king. A mud-splattered youth made his way purposefully the king. He knelt on one knee.

"Your Majesty." He ducked his head.

"What news?" Henry asked. He knew there wouldn't be any missive, nothing in writing. Oral news was always the most secure. If the messenger was killed en route, then the message

was lost with the messenger. Besides, he had long since instituted the use of Gaelic for sending important messages. Few
people outside of Scotland, unless they were Irish, knew the
language.

"My chief sends his regards, but believes it best to remain
hidden in the woods beyond," the scout replied. "The English
are moving into position as we speak and will soon be setting up
their camp just beyond the ramparts. The Murrays and the
Ogilvies have agreed to surround the camp with the intent of
laying siege once the English settle for the night. You will see
the banner across the fields. They plan to raise it high and light
it as a beacon, to announce the onslaught of their attack to the
troops here in the castle. There will be no further communication until the mission is complete. The English are thick as
thieves out there, Your Majesty."

"Yes, I'm sure they are. I shall have men watching for the
signal. Good job. You best stay here and fight from this end."

"Yes, Your Majesty."

"Robbie. Take the lad down to the kitchens. I'm sure the
cook has something to spare for our brave messenger."

"Yes, Your Majesty." Robbie led the lad out of the room as
Henry continued making plans for the castle frontal attack.

"And instruct the captain to secure all the entry points. All
gates and passageways must be sealed and heavily guarded."

"Yes, Your Majesty."

The men sat in silence for several minutes, the only sound
permeating the large room was the occasional rustle of shifting
feet, a few coughs and the spattering, crackling flames from the
fireplace. Ian was the first to speak. "So, the battle begins.
Surround and conquer."

Henry was startled by Ian's use of Bothwell's exact words,
but he didn't look up. Noticing his expression, Ian chuckled.
"We all know the famous Lord Bothwell's approach to dealing

with the English. He learned it from his peers. It's the Scottish way. Always has been."

"Aye. You're right. It is the Scottish way. I hadn't thought of those words in some time. There hasn't been a battle on Scottish soil in over a century." He had been intently studying his feet, for no particular reason other than to focus his thoughts. Looking up, his eyes caught the knowing look of his friend. "I didn't want to be the first monarch to start a new war with England."

"Well, you're not the first, lad." Ian said in little more than a whisper, meant for the king's ears alone. He frequently used the familiar when he was making light of something Henry said.

"The first in a long time, Ian. And I'm not sure this will bode well."

"We are strong, Your Majesty." He returned to the more formal address, since they were surrounded by a room full of loyal subjects. "We will prevail against the English menace. We always have."

"Aye. For now and forever."

"For now and forever." Mutterings around the room echoed the same Scottish battle cry, the one Henry's ancestor, Mary Elizabeth, had first uttered as she rallied her forces to keep Scotland independent and free.

"Ian. I need your men to add extra security at the entries and boost the manpower along the walls," Henry stated in his steady command voice. He had no choice but to face this unwelcome force head-on and fight he would, alongside his men. He wasn't one to shirk his duty and let others do the dirty work. "I have men already posted along the ramparts and, as you heard, orders are being executed to seal all entrances to the castle grounds."

"I'll get right to it, Your Majesty." Ian stood abruptly and waved to his men. "Thomas." A thick-set man in his mid-thirties made his way forward. He stood at least a couple of inches taller than Ian and had the weathered look of a seasoned battle commander. The Scots may not have had major scuffles with the English or any full-out war on their lands, but the ruling clans had their own little clashes here and there, maintaining their lands and protecting their own people. This man would know the terrain as well as the tactics to lead this siege to success. Alongside Henry's chosen captain, of course. "March the perimeter and station men as you see the need."

"Yes, my lord." Thomas nodded smartly and inclined his head towards his king. "Your Majesty." Just as abruptly, he waved his men out of the room to do as ordered. There were other MacGregors outside, probably stationed around the guardhouse square, warriors awaiting their orders. The guardhouse square had been Henry's idea to extend the battlements and provide the castle with an extra level of defense. He also had more ditches dug around the walls with a caponier, complete with musket openings to protect his troops while at the same time taking aim on the advancing enemy. Ian had suggested these additions to Stirling Castle and Henry was pleased he had listened to his friend's advice. It would serve them well in this upcoming battle.

Henry and Ian were alone. More or less. At least, momentarily. Heavy footsteps sounded like galloping horses as they approached the grand room. "Your Majesty." Robbie and the castle's captain, John Stirling, greeted the king in unison.

"Your Majesty." This time only John spoke. "The signal has been sighted. We have the drawbridge up and all entry points are well sealed and guarded. Shall I load the canon and rain down a barricade of canon balls on the poor English bastards?"

"Yes. Let the battle begin. The caponier is manned?"

"Yes, Your Majesty."

"Have they breached the River Forth?" Stirling Castle was

an important strategically situated castle, not only for its impenetrable height and steep climb from the surrounding countryside, but also because it controlled one of the main access crossings along the river which wove its way around the castle and the community, the River Forth.

"Not yet, Your Majesty. But they appear to be setting charges to blow the bridge."

"They must be stopped. We need the bridge. It's strategic to our plans. We must get word to Bruce and Wallace."

"I'm sure they are aware, Your Majesty," Ian pointed out. "As we all are. They will be taking steps to prevent the bridge's destruction."

"Aye. You're right, Ian."

"Top the canon and let them roar. Let's defend our castle, for whomever holds the keys to Stirling Castle holds the keys to Scotland. And we mustn't let the English have those keys."

"Aye." Ian, Robbie and John agreed unanimously. John bowed and made his exit to follow through with his orders.

Henry stood abruptly. "Well, Ian, Robbie, I believe it's time we took our place in the action, don't you think?"

"You shouldn't allow yourself to be seen, Your Majesty," Robbie advised. "You are a target."

"I shall stand well behind the canons and use my Ignazio Porro device to see all the action."

"You mean your binoculars?" Ian asked, his twinkled. He knew how his king loved to use the more formal names for new inventions. The binoculars weren't exactly new, but they had undergone some wonderful advancements and were excellent tools for situations like the one they were facing.

"Aye. Robbie. Fetch them for me and send my man in with my bulletproof vest, sword and bow and arrows. I'll be armed and dangerous. You'll see."

"Bulletproof vest?" Ian quirked an eyebrow. "This I have to

see. I heard about the Japanese invention using layers of silk to prevent bullets from piercing through to the skin. And it works?"

"So, they say. Hopefully we won't have to test the theory."

Robbie returned with the binoculars and Henry's man carrying the armor and weapons. Ian watched in awe as Henry slid into the vest and strapped on his sword belt. The king slipped the quiver of arrows over his shoulder.

"Impressive!" he said. "But why the bow and arrows?"

"You know I'm a good shot. And there's nothing better than a bow and arrow when fighting from the top of a castle wall. Wouldn't you agree, men?"

"Aye, Your Majesty," they spoked in unison.

"Rather archaic, though." Ian shook his head.

"Archaic? Perhaps. But effective? Definitely." Sword sheathed, quiver of arrows strapped over his back, he was ready. Taking the bow, he nodded to the men. "Besides, guns are not always as effective as we'd like them to be, especially from a distance." He waved his hand in the direction of the door. "Shall we? To the ramparts it is."

"Perhaps the tower of the caponier might be better," Ian suggested, lamely, as he knew Henry would object.

"No. I want to be outside. Above the action. With a clear view." He slapped Ian fondly on the back. "To the battlements, men."

Ian followed the king, shaking his head as he muttered, "Stubborn old..." He wasn't allowed to finished his grumblings.

"I heard you." Henry didn't break a stride as he called back over his shoulder. The two never did lose their love for bantering. "I'm not an old coot. Primarily because coot is an English expression and we don't use English expressions in the Scottish court."

"Yes, Your Majesty." Ian sounded suitably chastised.

The first boom of canon fire rattled the foundation. Henry quickened his pace, gripping the precious binoculars so they wouldn't fall from his grasp. He moved with military precision. The men exited the castle into the esplanade, making haste towards the stone steps leading up to the top of the walls where the canons sat in their casemates. Another canon let loose its ball as the men reached the top. The noise was deafening. The officer in charge of the men manning the canons nodded in acknowledgement as he noticed their presence. He didn't move, remaining in position at the end of the line of canons, shouting out orders.

Another canon boomed. Smoke emitted from the trajectory and more smoke was seen below where the canon ball had reached its target.

Henry made his way across the landing, coming to stand beside the officer shouting orders. Raising his binoculars to his eyes, he glanced through the lenses, over the man's shoulders, studying the smoking targets below. Between canon bursts, he asked, "Status?"

"We've managed to cause some damage to the enemy forces, Your Majesty." The answer was brief. Another order was barked. Another canon fired.

Across the smouldering targets, Henry could almost make out shadows of figures closing in on the English invaders. His men. His clans. His people. They were making their move to protect their homeland. To surround the enemy and expunge him. Bothwell's strategy of surround and conquer. The Scottish strategy.

The sounds of yelling, musket fire, orders shouted, swords clashing mixed with the intermittent boom of the canons. It became a blur of noise and smoke. Henry didn't like the battle-field. Too much pent-up anger exploding into nonsensical bloodshed. For what? But he knew there was no alternative.

Victoria had made it abundantly clear. He either fought the English or he lost his country. He could never live with the knowledge he had caused the demise of what centuries of Scottish monarchs had worked hard to build up and maintain.

A loud boom from below caused the foundation beneath their feet to tremble violently. "They have their canon in place and they're doing their own bit of damage, Your Majesty." The officer yelled in the king's ear. "You might be safer down below, Your Majesty."

Another explosion caused the stone foundation of the casement at the far end of the wall to crumble, taking the canon and its men to a crushing descent. The officer increased the rapidity of canon fires as much as he could given the time needed to reload after each firing. The Scottish canons continued to hit targets below. Suddenly, out of the smoke from the crumbling wall came a stream of men in English uniform. As they scrambled to get a footing, Ian called for his men to secure the ramparts.

Henry heard swords being drawn and started to draw his own, but before he had his weapon fully released, a sharp blast hit him in the shoulder. The pain cascaded throughout his body like fire. He'd been hit. By what, he couldn't ascertain. He heard the crash of glass as his binoculars fell from his grasp and shattered on the stone floor. He heard a voice, Ian's voice perhaps, penetrating his consciousness as it quickly ebbed away. "Your Majesty. Henry. The king." And all went black.

TWENTY-SIX

Secure Facility, Holyrood House, Year of Our Lord 2445

Voices trickled around him like a dizzying haze.

"We can't let him die. Not now."

"The future depends on him."

"Whose future? His? Or ours?"

"Both."

"And the boy?"

"Later. We must save King Henry first."

The fog closed in on him. For how long? He couldn't tell. When it cleared, he noticed sunlight trickling through curtains which must be as old and threadbare as he felt. He was sure they were the same curtains which lined the chambers in his time. Wasn't he still in his time? Everything was so different. The beeping, the smell of something potent, the constant clatter of footsteps marching up and down the hall beyond his room, marching to and around his bed. Puttering. Everyone was efficiently puttering at something. Who were these people in their stark white uniforms? He didn't know them. Or did he?

His eyes flickered open. Someone was fiddling with a tube draped from a pole. He felt a surge of something cold enter his arm. Looking down, he noticed tubing fastened to his arm. He tried to reach with the other arm to pull it out. It was invasive. His other arm struggled, but wouldn't budge. It was tied down. Why? Why was he confined in such a manner?

"Oh. You're awake, are you? I'll fetch the doctor." The female figure stopped her fussing and patted his arm. "Don't fuss. You're perfectly safe. These are just medicines to make you better. You almost died, you know. Gunshot grazed your heart. It stopped. The doctor here is a whiz. He patched you up and kept your heart pumping."

"My binoculars." Why was he worrying about something so inconsequential when he was lying in a bed, strapped in securely, presumably sometime far in the future.

"You mean these?" The woman held up what might have been his binoculars. It was a crumpled mess, but then his eyes weren't focussing too well. "Interesting contraption. Binoculars, you say. They're much more sophisticated nowadays."

He glanced at her. "What year is it?"

"I guess it doesn't matter if I tell you. They'll wipe your memory before sending you back." She appeared to be studying him intently. "2445. And, yes, this is your home, your Holyrood House. Though sometime in the last century, it was converted into a research facility. Very secret."

"2445. That's over 500 years from my time!" He shook his head in disbelief. Was he dreaming? This couldn't be possible. "Holyrood House a research facility. And you said they'd wipe my memory. Who? Why? All of it?"

"Enough, nurse." The male voice from across the room startled them. Henry recognized the voice. He couldn't place it. Where had he heard it before? Certainly not in this time. 2445? Is it possible? He'd never jumped so far into the future before. "Leave us." The man's voice was closer. "Now. You'll be disciplined later." Disciplined? For what?

"Yes, doctor." She gave Henry a final pat on the arm and marched out of the room.

"Well, King Henry I. You gave us all quite a scare. We have to get you up on your feet again. You still have work to do in the nineteenth-century. Without your work, there will be no such facility as the one in which we are now." The doctor stood at the end of the bed, studying the man lying prone. A forced smile marred the doctor's face as he took a look at the black device he held in his hand. Presumably a chart, some sort of record of Henry's progress. "The nurse spoke too freely. But she's right. It won't matter. Not after we inject the memory block."

"No. I want to remember." Henry struggled to sit up, but the restraints kept him immobile. "I want to understand, to appreciate what is going on here and what I need to do in my time."

"Too much information of the future can be a dangerous tool, King Henry. Especially for someone in your position of power and authority." The doctor walked around to the side of the bed and started poking and prodding the patient. "Yet, in spite of all our advances in science and medicine, we still have to poke and prod our patients to get a clearer sense of what's going on underneath."

Henry grimaced as he endured the examination. The doctor undid the restricting straps binding Henry to the bed. He stretched the king's arms, then his legs, bending and pulling. He prodded the abdomen and listened, presumably, to his heart.

"It's a stethoscope, isn't it?" Henry asked, pointing at the device. He knew they existed. They had been around for most of his era. He'd never seen one being used, since he'd never been deathly ill before. Nor injured.

"Yes." The doctor pulled the ends from his ears and then noted something on his black box. "I guess they were still relatively new in your timeline. They have improved considerably over the centuries, but never replaced. A valuable tool for listening to a person's heart and lungs."

"What are you holding in your hand?" Henry was full of questions. So much of what he was seeing was foreign to him.

"An electronic device which monitors and records your vital signs." The doctor held it so Henry could see a screen full of numbers, codes and comments. "In your era, the doctor would write this information on a paper chart that was kept in the room, usually at the end of the patient's bed. Paper is a precious commodity in the twenty-fifth century as there are very few trees left on our planet to sustain the production of paper."

"No trees?" Henry was shocked at the prospect. "What about forests? And wildlife?"

The doctor shook his head sadly. "No. I've never seen a tree in this era, other than in history books. Everything is all concrete, metal and skyscrapers. Nothing green or colorful to be seen. And what you refer to as wildlife? Gone. Extinct. We don't even have domesticated animals. And don't get me going on the idea of farms. All gone."

"What!" Henry was the one to shake his head this time. In disbelief. "Then what do you eat?"

"Synthetically prepared energy drinks. We all consume the same daily. No hunger. No obesity. No illness. Just overpopulation and long life."

Henry tried to absorb this information. He couldn't comprehend a life without nature, animals, trees, farms, and, of course, real food. "What happened? How did humans evolve to this kind of madness?"

It was as if something had snapped in the doctor's conscious. He suddenly straightened his shoulders. "Enough. This conversation is irrelevant. You need to have your memories erased." He reached into the cabinet beside the bed and pulled out a long-needled syringe, already loaded with some sort of cocktail.

Henry wanted no part of whatever was in the needle. His arms were still free. The doctor had neglected to refasten his restrains. Or had he forgotten? No time to lose. He reached over and grabbed the doctor's wrists, wrenching the syringe from his hands. Instead of knocking it to the ground, he took control of it. Before the startled doctor could react in self defense, Henry stuck the needle in the doctor's arm and pushed the juice into its target. The doctor crumbled to the floor at the side of the bed. Henry replaced the syringe in the doctor's hands so it would look like the task had been successfully completed.

After a few minutes, Henry called out, "Nurse. Nurse. Help." He loosely refastened his restraints and lay down as if the doctor had just finished examining him. "Nurse. Help." He must have called several times before the door opened and the same nurse who had treated him earlier entered the room.

"Oh my!" she gasped, seeing the doctor lying on the floor. "What happened?"

"I don't know." Henry was playing the role of a mind-washed idiot. At least, he hoped he was sounding like he'd had his memory wiped. "I just heard a crash and noticed this man lying on the floor next to me. Who is he? Who are you? Do I know you? Where am I?"

The nurse didn't look entirely convinced with Henry's acting skills, but she made herself busy. She called into some black device fastened to her shoulder, requesting assistance and then knelt beside the doctor to feel his pulse. "He's not breathing."

Henry closed his eyes, focused on his time and vanished.

TWENTY-SEVEN

Stirling Castle, After the Battle, Year of Our Lord 1875

Henry gasped.

"He's waking." Ian's voice. It sounded far away.

The king's eyes cracked open. The light stunned him and he closed them. He heard voices all around him, some close, some further away.

"Henry."

"Your Majesty."

"I think he's going to be all right."

It was hard to distinguish who was speaking, but the voices were all male.

He pulled his eyes open a little wider. Blinked. Shut them again.

Another cough. This one deeper, forcing his eyes to open fully. He blinked rapidly as he allowed the fog to clear.

"Where am I?" he croaked. He tried to say more, but another cough interrupted. His mouth was dry. Like sandpaper.

A hand took his and held it firmly. "You're in your chambers, Your Majesty." It sounded like his doctor, David Aitken.

"What happened?" His voice was a little stronger this time.

His eyes were starting to focus, to make out the figures around him. Dr. Aitken was closest, a finger underneath the wrist, his mouth forming numbers. He was counting. Checking the king's pulse.

Ian stood just behind the doctor. "You gave us quite a scare, Your Majesty." He had reverted to the more formal address. "You took a bullet in the shoulder as the enemy stormed the castle. Your fall backwards on the battlements knocked you out cold."

"But my vest?" Henry sputtered. "It was supposed to stop bullets from penetrating."

"And it might have done so, but the bullet, or whatever it was, found a weak spot." The doctor touched Henry's shoulder, gently, but the king flinched anyway.

"What do you mean by 'whatever it was'?" Henry glanced around at the mirage of faces who, in turn, were studying him intently.

After a few minutes of stalling, Ian took the initiative to explain. "We don't know what or who they were that scaled the ramparts, Your Majesty. They were all dressed in black body armor of some description and their weapons were nothing like I've ever seen before. Your bulletproof vest was no match for whatever they shot into your body. Even the explosion which breeched the castle walls was done by something otherworldly."

"It's like a magical force appeared out of nowhere," Wallace added. The Scots had their little people and their bits of magic, but they were a sturdy lot, well grounded in reality. They were not ones to have fanciful notions, but this certainly sounded like fanciful thoughts, even for an Ogilvie.

"And they all vanished as soon as they saw you fall." Bruce snapped his fingers to emphasize his point. "Just like that." He was shaking his head as if he still didn't believe what he had seen. Which he didn't believe. Not at all. Even though he was not alone in witnessing the onslaught. "We all saw it." They nodded their heads in unison. "We managed to capture one of the men, if you could call him a man. But even he vanished before we could lock him in the dungeons."

Silence ensued. The king allowed the words of his most valiant men to sink in. What were they dealing with here? Another force from the future? Finally, "How long have I been out?" He spoke through clenched teeth, barring his frustration at being, once again, at a loss to understand what had just transpired.

"Several hours. All night, actually. We contained the breech and overcame the enemy. All is well. The wretched English lord now festers in the dungeons below."

Henry wanted to laugh, but it came out as a bark. His mouth was so dry. "Water." Ian moved around behind the doctor and lifted Henry's head, helping him sip from a cup. Mouth moistened, he spoke. "I knew there was a reason to maintain those medieval dungeons."

Ian was the only one to catch Henry's attempt at wry humor. He chuckled softly. "Aye, Your Majesty."

The room was coming into better focus. Henry felt the stitch in his shoulder where the bullet had entered. He forced himself into a sitting position. Slowly. The room started to sway. He paused. Breathed deeply. Clenched his eyes. Opened them again and pushed himself up further.

"Are the ships ready?" Henry asked Ian. "Where's the Admiral?"

"He's back." Ian flashed a smile over his shoulder at the others before addressing his king's questions. "The ships are ready, Your Majesty. Admiral McKay is awaiting orders to proceed."

"His Majesty needs to rest," the doctor advised.

"I've rested enough. We're at war, Doctor. There's no rest

for the weary when we have a war to fight. You may leave us."
He waved the doctor away. When the doctor was out of earshot
and his chambers were only occupied by himself and his most
trusted chiefs, Henry spoke. "Bruce. Wallace." He motioned for
the Murray and the Ogilvie chiefs to step closer. They placed
themselves in a semicircle around the king's bed, Ian on one
side, Bruce on the other and Wallace at the foot of the bed.

"Send them." Henry gave his first command to Ian, who
knew what Henry wanted done. They had discussed it at great
length before the battle. He explained the tactic to the others.
"Send the ships. We need to catch the English at sea. Unawares.
Capture their ships and commandeer them for our own use."

"Do we have enough ships to surround the English?" Bruce
asked, a look of concern etching his brow. "The last thing we
need is for the English to take what ships we have to use against
us."

"We have enough." Henry spoke with confidence. "And we
have the advantage of surprise on our side. They won't be
expecting us. They know little or nothing of our seafaring readi-
ness. We will capture the English ships as they leave or enter
English ports and we'll cut off their trade routes. The captured
English ships will be added to our fleet. We also have our own
trading vessels which are due to return from the colonies any
day now. We have enough. Admiral McKay is at the ready.
Once he receives my orders, our plan will be set in motion."

"And the wall?" Wallace was asking about Hadrian's Wall,
the historic Roman wall which marked the border between
England and Scotland.

"The Lowlanders have already been dispatched to secure its
length," Ian took the initiative to answer. "No one will be
allowed access across the Wall for some time to come. The
orders are to shoot first, ask questions later. I'll be joining them
as soon as I've passed on the orders to Admiral McKay."

"And us, Your Majesty?" Bruce asked. "What will you have us do?"

"The northern ports need to be strengthened with additional manpower," Henry continued. "Make sure there is more than adequate fighting men at every possible point of access from the water. But keep the men hidden as best you can. Secure the lookouts and be prepared to ambush whoever dares trying to land on our shores."

"Yes, Your Majesty." The vote was unanimous. No one would dare challenge their king. Suggestions could be made, but they didn't appear to be necessary. Henry had everything well planned. In spite of his recent injuries, in spite of his regaining consciousness only a short time ago, Henry was prepared and ready to lay out the next initiative. He was a good strategist.

"And you, Your Majesty? Where will you be?"

"Here and there." He noticed the looks shooting from one chief to the other. "Well guarded at all times, my friends. So, don't worry. I'll keep Ian close at hand. Others too. I want to check on my dear wife and make sure the castle at Loch Leven is impenetrable. All I need at this moment would be for her to escape and wreak more havoc."

"And your son?"

"Safe."

"Now. Bruce. Wallace. Before you leave. Assign trusted men to question the prisoners and have the English lord shackled and brought to me at once."

"Yes, Your Majesty."

"Ian."

"Yes, Your Majesty."

"Remain here, but hidden. I want you to hear everything. In case I forget or the prisoner gets out of hand."

"Yes, Your Majesty." Knowing the secret hiding places as

well as the king, Ian slid into the alcove behind the curtains and settled in to wait and to listen.

Alone at last, Henry continued sitting on the side of his bed. He didn't want the others to know, but the room was still swimming around him. Between the battle, the injury and the jump to the future, which had ended in yet another confrontation, Henry's mind was abuzz with ponderings and concerns.

What was his injury? Why did it require a skip to the future to heal? Had he come so perilously close to death? Why were the people of the twenty-fifth century so concerned about keeping him alive? What was his role in all this time travel nonsense? Why did they want to block his memories? What else had he learned from the future? What details had been disturbingly erased from his mind? Or had it been erased? Was there some remnant memory yet to resurface?

Footsteps could be heard approaching, the rattle of chains indicating a prisoner, or at least a person in chains, being escorted to him. The English Lord. Henry stood and grabbed the robe he always draped over a chair near the bed. He had just slipped his feet in his slippers and shrugged on the robe when a knock sounded.

"Enter." He walked to the window, tying his robe closed before pulling the drapes aside. Knowing Ian was hiding, he was careful not to pull the drapes all the way. It was dawn. He wanted some light. Natural light. The sun was rising, glistening mightily over the ramparts below. He heard the rattle of chains as the door opened and the prisoner was shuffled inside.

TWENTY-EIGHT

"Your Majesty." The man leading the prisoner bowed his head, the predominantly deep blue tartan with green and red interweaving the plaid, swayed with his movement as he stepped away from his prisoner and stood by the door. It was one of Bruce's men. A Murray. Henry couldn't remember the name, but he knew the voice. "Shall I stay, Your Majesty?"

"No. It's not necessary." He waved the man off.

"I'll be just outside the door if you need me, Your Majesty." The man bowed again and left, closing the door behind him.

"The tables are turned now, aren't they, Lord Dudley. Or shall I just call you Arthur?"

The man who stood before him was shackled and filthy. His clothes, once fine as befitting an English lord, were torn and dirtied from battle and from the dungeon. Henry wouldn't be at all surprised to hear some of his men had taken pleasure in giving him a beating on the way to the dungeons. He didn't like the idea, but these things happened.

Lord Dudley, Arthur, glared at the Scottish king. He didn't speak. He didn't pay proper homage to the royal personage standing before him.

"Lost your tongue?" Henry considered pacing, as he usually did when faced with a problem. The room was still spinning and the last thing he needed was to pass out before his prisoner. He simply crossed his arms and returned stare for stare, silently, allowing the power of silence to engulf the man before him, to unsettle his opponent.

"You have no idea what you're up against." The words were spoken with sinister undertones.

"Are you threatening me?" Henry raised an eyebrow, mimicking an aura of surprise. "You're hardly in a position to threaten me."

"It's not me you need to worry about." The sinister intonation remained.

"Oh. Right. My cousin, the Queen of England. I'll have you know we've already chatted. She knows where I stand. And, as for retaliation, we have our own little surprise set in motion. It's been planned and executed in anticipation since the day my wife was imprisoned."

"If that's the case, then how is it that my men and I were able to sneak into the country?" He sneered. "Not only that, we were able to traipse into Edinburgh and Holyrood House with little resistance. And we made it to the walls of Stirling Castle and managed to breech it. Something no one else in history has ever done."

"We have our flaws, but the error has been addressed. We learn from our mistakes."

"So, you say. Until you fall for another mistake in judgement."

"For someone bound in shackles and looking a little worse for wear, you seem pretty sure of yourself and your so-called English cause. Did it ever occur to you, or you countrymen, this simple fact: Scotland doesn't want anything to do with the English? Not now. Not ever." The room was steadying, so he started to pace. Around his prisoner, keeping an eye on the man and his features from all angles, looking for a sign of weakness. "I don't understand why the English think they can rule the Scots. We have fought viciously over the centuries, and often won, long before the Romans walked this continent. Perhaps you can enlighten me on this intense obsession with owning and controlling Scotland. Perhaps you can explain the English people's desperate need to abduct my son."

Henry had come full circle and was now standing inches from Arthur, face-to-face. The once proud, and tall, imposing figure of the English lord had shrivelled to the point where he appeared to be no taller than Henry.

"Because we can." The lord spat in Henry's face. The king didn't flinch or bat an eye. The spittle trickled down his cheek. He allowed it. Ignored it. He just stared. Emboldened, the Arthur carried his thoughts further. "Because we can and we will. Scotland was meant to be ours. With your son, brought up English and married to an English princess, there will be no further opposition. Especially with you out of the way permanently. Scotland should have been ours when James succeeded Elizabeth."

Henry stepped back, shaking his head slowly so as not to unsettle his equilibrium in the process of demonstrating his disbelief. "It didn't belong to you then and it doesn't belong to you now. James had no right to attempt to force the amalgamation. Scotland didn't want anything to do with England. Not then. Not now. Not ever. My ancestor was only interested in more power. As is my cousin. We will maintain our independence, Arthur." He managed to keep his eyes rivetted on his prisoner. "We will succeed and we will remain independent. Scotland, strong and free. For now and forever."

Arthur snorted. "You think some meagre Scottish battle cry will prevent the English from taking power? The more resistance you demonstrate, the more brutality which will follow. We English don't take resistance lightly."

"Don't I know it. I've seen how you people brutalize others in your colonies. It's not our way and it never will be." He took another step back. Keeping his eyes on Arthur, he called in a booming voice, "Guards."

His chamber doors opened almost instantly. "Take the prisoner away."

Arthur held back before he was dragged from the room. "Like I said, Your Majesty," he almost spat the last words. "You don't know what or who you are dealing with. Rest assured, for now and forever will be your last battle cry."

"We shall see about that," Henry called out to the retreating figure.

TWENTY-NINE

Secure Facility, Holyrood House, Year of Our Lord 2445

"Father. Help me." It was Edward. His son. He was calling to him. He didn't know how it was he recognized the boy's voice. The last time he'd visited Edward, the boy was still an infant. But somehow he knew. Father's intuition? Perhaps.

What was Edward doing here? In this place? In this time? They weren't implanting him, were they? Why?

Henry forced his eyes open, forced them to focus. He was in the room again. He wasn't alone. There was another bed. Next to his. A small figure writhed and tossed on its surface.

"Edward?"

"Father."

Henry felt the restraints as he struggled to move. All he could do was turn his head, marginally at best. He studied the boy in the bed next to him. Not the baby he had left with his great ancestors in the twenty-first century a short time ago. Or was it? Time traveling was a complication of time. Mind boggling. This lad must be about ten. Thinking back to his youth, it made sense. He was about ten when he had his first time travel adventure.

"Edward." He tried to sound reassuring. He knew the boy

must be terrified. He had been. "It's going to be okay. You're safe." At least for now, he thought to himself. "I'm here." If only he could slip his hand out of the restraints and reach across the chasm separating the two beds. Holding his son's hand might be reassuring for them both.

"I can't move, Father. What's happening?"

Just then the door opened and what appeared to be a doctor entered followed by a couple of male nurses. Or so he thought. Appearances could be deceiving.

"You're awake." The doctor was abrupt. "I'm not taking any chances with you this time, King Henry." He waggled a finger accusingly at Henry. "You knocked me out cold the last time you were here."

The memory trickled at the back of his brain. A glimpse and then it was gone, as if he had reached out to catch a moonbeam and it vanished before his fist could close around it. Other memories flashed through his head.

Implants.

Twenty-fifth century.

Memory-erasing drugs.

"Why do you keep bringing me back?" Henry asked. "If you would just give me some answers."

"Answers I do have, Your Majesty." The doctor was holding a syringe, preparing the contents for injection. "But not in this time period. When we meet again, I'll explain."

"What are you doing to my son?"

The needle went into his arm and everything went black.

THIRTY

Toronto, Summer, Year of Our Lord 2030

"Father. You came. I knew you would come."

"Happy birthday, Edward," Henry greeted his son, returning the bear hug as the boy launched himself into his arms. Holding the boy back to study him intently, Henry said, *"My, you have grown."*

"I'm twelve today, Father. Did you bring me something? A gift? Grandmother Marie has made my favorite supper and there's cake. Chocolate. My favorite." He identified his two ancestors, his caregivers, as grandmother with their given names to distinguish which grandmother was which.

"Mine, too. And, yes, I have a gift." He left the boy to retrieve the items he had brought with him, but left at the door. He picked up a long parcel and laughed as he noticed his son's eyes pop wide open in surprised anticipation.

"What is it?"

"Well. Open it and see for yourself."

Edward didn't wait for his grandmothers to appear. He merely crouched on the floor in the middle of the hall and tore at the paper. Opening the package, he exclaimed a simple, expressive, "Oh!" He pulled out the contents. "My very own bow and arrows and a quiver. You've heard how well I shoot the arrows. Grandmother Mary Elizabeth has been teaching me, using hers. But they're old. Very old."

Henry laughed. "Yes, they are. But so are these. New, but also old. I'm glad you like archery and I'm pleased to hear you're so good at it. You never know when a good arrow shot will protect you from the invading forces."

"Yes, Father. Thank you."

"Keep practising. And take good care of them."

"Yes, Father." Edward ran his fingers along the back of the bow, admiring its feel. "Are you taking me with you this time?"

Edward had been told of his heritage and the time travel history of his father and two grandmothers. Knowing his place in history, he was anxious to return to his time and stand at his father's side. He had never met his mother. He only knew she was a traitor and she had died in prison a few years earlier. He didn't mourn her. He couldn't mourn someone he didn't know, someone who had threatened his father, his family and his heritage.

"Henry," Grandmother Marie stood at the doorway leading to the kitchen from which tempting aromas permeated. For a many-centuries' old queen, she appeared to be no more than sixty. For a member of royalty, pampered from the day she was born, she certainly didn't look the part. Hair disheveled, a flour-dusted apron draped around a casual outfit of this century called jeans and a t-shirt, much like his son was wearing, she certainly didn't look like a woman with a past.

"Grandmother Marie." Henry made his way over to the woman who, as far as he knew, was the first in this long line of time traveling royals. The changes they'd made, before his time and during his time, were astronomical. The history books wouldn't record those changes. The history books were different *too, altered by the time changes marked on the pages.* "*Where's Grandmother Mary Elizabeth?*" *He was pleased to have both his many great grandmothers care for his son's safekeeping and education. It was difficult coming to terms with what times his ancestors came from in this current future time. Grandmother Marie had tried to explain how it was during the years leading up to Queen Elizabeth's death and the attempt to amalgamate Scotland with England. Grandmother Mary Elizabeth had hidden in the far north of Scotland, but had spent much of her time jumping around time to spy and to help. Like here. Like now. With young Edward. His son.*

"*Coming.*" *Her voice could be heard from deep within the kitchen.*

"*She's trying to put icing on Edward's birthday cake. A special design.*" *Grandmother Marie rolled her eyes.* "*It's more like she's decorating the kitchen than the cake. There's icing and sugar everywhere.*"

"*What's so special about this cake?*"

"*It's a superhero cake.*" *Edward beamed at his father.* "*Look Grandmother Marie. My very own bow and arrows.*"

"*Yes, I see.*"

"*Superhero?*" *Henry quirked an eyebrow.* "*Who or what is this superhero?*"

They were interrupted by the sound of the doorbell. Henry jumped. Grandmother Marie just chuckled. She understood the sounds of the twenty-first century. Henry was still acclimatizing himself, one short visit at a time.

"*If you stay long enough,*" *Edward whispered to his father,* "*I'll show you a superhero.*"

Henry managed a quick smile for his son before turning his attention to the front door. The voice, a man's voice, greeted Grandmother Marie startling him. He recognized it, but he couldn't place it. His great ancestor stepped back and allowed the man to enter. When Henry saw the figure step into the hall, he gasped.

"You!" He pointed a finger at him accusingly. "What are you doing here? You can't take him. You can't." He positioned himself in front of Edward, trying to block access to his son.

"That's Uncle Cecil, Father. I told you about him." Edward slipped past his father and ran to the man at the door.

"Uncle Cecil?" Henry shook his head in disbelief. This wasn't any uncle or relation to either himself or his son. Or was he? The man was the doctor from the future. Was it possible he was also a descendant of his?

Uncle Cecil caught Edward as he launched himself into a big hug. The two laughed as the older man picked up the boy and tossed him in the air. "Twelve years old. And you still like to fly."

"I'll always like flying, Uncle Cecil," Edward continued to giggle as he was placed firmly on the floor once again.

"Well, happy birthday, young man."

"Look at what my father gave me." Edward, not one to stand still for a minute, dashed back to his father, where he had left his gift lying on the floor. He took it to his uncle and showed off the fine qualities.

Uncle Cecil demonstrated his admiration of the gift. "A fine gift for a talented archer." He was giving it a seal of approval. As if it was needed. All it mattered was what Edward thought.

As if sensing Henry's discomfort with his presence, the so-called uncle patted Edward on the head and walked over to the boy's father. "Your Majesty. We meet again." He confirmed Henry's suspicions. "Yes. I am Doctor Stuart of the twenty-fifth century. I am also Doctor Stuart of the twenty-first century. And I am a direct descendant of the royal Stuarts. Of you, and Marie and Mary Elizabeth. And all those in between."

"You can't have him, Doctor Stuart!" It was all Henry could think to say. "You can't implant my son. You took advantage of the rest of us. But I won't allow you to take advantage of my son."

"Please call me Cecil." The doctor let out a deep sigh. "There's nothing I can do. He's already had the implant inserted."

"What!" Henry was astounded. Angry. "How dare you! When?"

"You were there."

"Gentlemen," Grandmother Marie scolded. "Little ears." She nodded at Edward.

"I have big ears now, Grandmother Marie." Edward was too smart to be placated. "What do you mean by implants? I want to know."

"Now look what you've done." It was Grandmother Mary Elizabeth standing behind them at the end of the hall. "Upset our birthday boy. Dinner is ready. Let's celebrate the young man's birthday and talk about this later."

"But I want to know!" Edward stomped his foot. He was used to getting what he wanted.

"And you will, son," Henry patted the lad on the shoulder. "And hopefully we all will understand what has been hidden from us for so long."

Edward led the way into the dining room and took his place at the head of the table. He was, after all, the birthday boy and deserved the place of honor. He eyed his cake with eager anticipation, marveling in Grandmother Mary Elizabeth's interpretation of a scene from one of Edward's comic book heroes.

"See, Father." He leaned over the table to point at things on the cake. "There's the hero fighting the evil menace with marvelous, high-tech weapons."

"So, this hero of yours is a good man?" Henry half stated, half asked, quirking an eyebrow as he concentrated on his son's soliloquy.

"Of course." Edward spoke as if everyone should know about superheroes. "He fights all the bad guys and makes the world a safer place. He has all kinds of cool gadgets and weapons, too."

"I'm sure he does." Henry stifled a chuckle by clearing his voice. "Now perhaps you should sit back in your seat like a gentleman so we can enjoy this wonderful feast your grandmothers have prepared for us."

"Yes Father." Edward sat back in his seat with obvious reluctance. "That's a great cake, Grandmother Mary Elizabeth. Thank you."

Grandmother Mary Elizabeth was obviously pleased with the praise. Henry beamed at his son's fine display of good manners. He would make a fine king one day. He should make a visit to the future and see for himself.

They enjoyed the good food and festivities, allowing the conversation to skirt around the topic of time travel and implants. Edward talked about his friends at school and what he was learning.

"I read about the war with the English, Father." He had blown out his birthday candles and, with Grandmother Marie's help, he was cutting into the cake, giving everyone ample portions of the sweet concoction. "Good bye superhero's City. Until next year." He bemoaned as the cake and the mythic city took the brunt of Edward's knife.

"And what did you learn?" Henry asked, anxious to know the history he had yet to experience.

"It was a long war and you almost lost." Edward took a mouthful of his cake. "Mmm! This is good, Grandmother Mary Elizabeth. The best cake you've made yet."

"Thank you, Edward." Grandmother Mary Elizabeth took a mouthful and nodded in agreement. "I have to agree with you. It is rather good."

Compliments scattered around the table as the family members present took one bit after another.

"How long was the war?" Henry returned the conversation to Edward's discussion about the war with the English.

"Six years." Edward spoke with his mouth full.

"Don't talk with your mouth full, Edward," Grandmother Marie scolded.

He swallowed deeply before answering. "Yes, Grandmother Marie."

"Six years! Why so long? And how did we almost lose?"

So many questions. Cecil interrupted. "Perhaps it's best if you don't know too much. You may change history for the worse."

"Or I may change history for the better as Grandmother Mary Elizabeth did," Henry argued. "We all make choices in life and then we have to live with our choices."

"And what would your choice be?" Cecil glanced across the table at the king.

THIRTY-ONE

Kirkwall Castle, Orkney Islands, Northern Scotland, Winter, Year of Our Lord 1877

Henry paced before the frost crusted window. It had been over a year since the first battle at Stirling. He had used his navy well to cut off trade and commerce to and from England, but it hadn't been enough. The English were resourceful if nothing else. Their vessels managed to make it around the outer perimeter of Ireland and up the coast to Scotland's far northern ports. Not an easy route, especially in the unseasonable weather which plagued the winter months specifically, but also most of the year. They had tried to get a foothold of the country from the north, but Henry had been forewarned. He was always prepared for the worse case scenario.

Here he was at Kirkwall Castle on the Orkeny Islands, in the middle of a blizzard, no less. His great ancestor, Queen Mary Elizabeth, had hidden well in this castle until the death of her cousin, Queen Elizabeth I, in 1603. Is this what he was doing now? Hiding?

"Father." The voice of his son startled him.

He stopped his pacing and faced the sound of the voice.

"Edward. What are you doing here? How did you..." He didn't finish his question. He saw the shadow of another person standing behind his son. The two moved closer, standing next to the fire blazing in the hearth, the light of the flames illuminating their presence with deep shadows. "Cecil?"

The man held up his hand to ward off further questions. "I couldn't let him come alone, Your Majesty. He's still fairly new to this time traveling gig, but he was determined to make this jump. To warn you. Something he read in his history book, about this ongoing war of yours."

"But, I don't understand." Henry moved from the window and came to stand next to his son. "You told me it wasn't wise to know too much from the future as it could drastically change things."

"And so it can." Cecil took a seat, not waiting for formal protocol to allow him the privilege. He crossed his legs and made himself comfortable. "This battle you're fighting with the English is not just with the enemy of your time. There are English forces from the future, from my time, from the twenty-fifth century. They are aiding the English forces of your time. Haven't you wondered at some of the victories? The battle at Stirling, your first battle. How did they breach the wall so easily? And the warriors that climbed over the barricade first weren't from your time. The weapon used to shoot you, was more powerful than any bulletproof vest of your era could protect."

"And their ability to appear out of nowhere," Henry added. "There's English forces marching across the island as we speak. Set to destroy this castle and me along with it."

"And to steal Scotland from the Scottish," Cecil added. "If this isn't stopped, then Scotland of the future definitely won't be the same. In Edward's twenty-first century, this upcoming battle ensured English victory and his Scotland of the twenty-first century didn't exist at all."

"But how do I stop a power with weapons beyond my understanding?" Henry took a seat opposite Cecil. He placed his elbows on his knees and leaned forward to rest his head in his hands.

"Come with me to the future, Henry. The battle you fight now has its origins in the twenty-fifth century. In order to win this battle, you'll have to fight it in another time." Cecil wasn't sure if his suggestions were making an impact. Henry continued to sit silently pondering his choices. "Your descendant, Queen Mary Elizabeth II, awaits you and all the time travelers of your family. Only you and your time traveling family can change things in the future to make things better for Scotland, both in the future and in the past. Together, you'll find a way and make a difference. Queen Mary Elizabeth II, the queen of my era, is as strong, as determined and as powerful as her namesake."

"But you said Scotland doesn't exist in the twenty-first century?" Henry countered, looking confused. "And, if it doesn't exist in the twenty-first century, how can it possibly exist in the twenty-fifth century?"

"We Scots are not so easy to wipe out, Your Majesty," Cecil replied. "There has always been a ready and waiting under-ground army and a king or queen ready to take the helm. It hasn't been easy. Especially lately with this newly perfected time travel implant. One I invented, I might add. Invented for the sole purpose of making sure Scotland never does become the vassal of England."

"Father." The boy was standing next to Henry, patting his arm. "Father. What Cecil says is true. The history books I have to study in the twenty-first century record stories of an unspeak-able force which almost annihilates the Scottish population, allowing the English free rein to move in and take over. The war has already lasted more than a year in your time. Our time." He quickly corrected himself. "And you, our people, don't seem to be making any headway. Am I correct?"

Henry nodded sadly, taking his son's hands in his. Following a deep, prolonged sigh, he spoke. "Edward. Cecil. I have to admit I wondered at the power and the strange abilities of the English invaders. But if this force we're fighting is from the twenty-fifth century, why didn't they just wipe us out when the war began. Or before that? Centuries before when Queen Mary Elizabeth took the crown of Scotland from her brother?"

"There were powers at war in the twenty-fifth century which slowed their progress in your time and in earlier times," Cecil explained. "And, they were advised to keep things low key so as not to raise suspicions from people like you who moved through time. They're starting to get frantic, though. And through their impatience to succeed, dire consequences will be felt in your country. They're making mistakes. Deadly mistakes. Dangerous mistakes. In our country. You must act fast. You must make your decision now. There's no time to waste."

"Frantic about what?" Henry snapped. He wasn't one to snap. He seldom lost his temper, but his frustration had reached an all time peak and he wanted answers. He wanted to understand. He hated not understanding what was going on around him.

His friend, Walter Scott, author *par excellence*, had warned him over and over again. "Scotland was a prize the English wanted to win, for no particular purpose than to win the prize." Walter had written several treatises singing the praises of his country: "its beauty unmatched anywhere in the world and a strong people who dedicated their lives to protecting and preserving this beauty." Henry particularly loved the man's writing. A phrase which immediately came to mind, one he had memorized for its eloquent beauty for times such as this, "O, what a tangled web we weave when first we practise to deceive!" Granted these words were written in an earlier time frame when Walter penned his poem, "Marion" in 1808. Walter was only a friend to Henry when the king jumped back in time for a visit and some literary consolation. Henry loved his literature and he loved the writings of Walter Scott. How apropos was this one simple line from the poem, especially given the circumstances, given his current predicament.

"Let's go, but Edward must return to the twenty-first century and his grandmothers." Henry was insistent. He wanted his son safe. Regardless of the outcome, the future of Scotland was in Edward's hands as much as it was in his.

Cecil and Edward both shook their heads. "Edward must come, too," Cecil stated firmly. "His presence is crucial to this mission's success."

"But why?"

"Because of what he knows." Cecil was brief. "And his implant is working differently from yours. It protects him from memory loss. You have managed to overcome the memory loss drugs we administered to aid you in forgetting what you saw in the twenty-fifth century. To a point. You don't remember everything, but enough to put the pieces together. Edward has a much stronger mind than that. And it works with the implant. Or, I should say the implant works with his mind, making it more resilient and resistant to memory-loss drugs."

"And this helps how?" Henry quirked an eyebrow, his lack of conviction obvious. "And how does it protect my son? Without him, Scotland has no future. You do realize that?"

"I do," Cecil nodded his head. "In more ways than you realize. Which is why I understand the importance of Edward accompanying us on this mission."

"Father," Edward spoke up before Henry could say more. "It's important. I know what the history books say. You don't as it hasn't happened yet. I know I can help. I've already done some jumps with both grandmothers. I have been to the Holyrood House Facility of the twenty-fifth century. I have not forgotten any of it, in spite of the drugs injected into my system. I have met Queen Mary Elizabeth II. And I have snooped the English royal court of the time period in question. I know what I'm doing. And I have a pretty good idea what needs doing."

Henry was stunned. He quirked an eyebrow and studied his son intently. What happened to the little boy whose twelfth birthday he had celebrated in the future? Even though, in this time, he wouldn't be twelve yet. Here he was, just twelve, ready to do battle. Not just in Henry's time, but well into the future as well.

"Very well," he spoke with harbored reluctance. "What do we need to bring in terms of weapons?"

"Whatever your preference." Cecil stood and walked closer to the fire, rubbing his hands together to store its warmth. "Edward has his bow and arrow." The boy held up the bow his father had given him on his birthday. "I believe your preference is the sword, or dirk as the old Scots called it."

"And a pistol." Henry patted his side where the pistol was inserted ready to be retrieved at a moment's notice. "Anything else? Won't our weapons seem pitiful when pitted against the weapons of your century?"

"True enough," Cecil swiveled around to face the king. "But you will be provided with what you need when we meet the queen. And, too much confidence in modern weaponry can be a hindrance."

"Too much confidence at any time or place can be one's downfall," Henry agreed. "Very well. Let's be on our way."

Cecil held up his hands. "Not so fast. We have a journey to make first. To the past. To understand the powers we're up against. These English warriors of the twenty-fifth century made their first appearance, that we know of, when Queen Mary Elizabeth, as a princess, first appeared in the sixteenth century. Right about the time of Queen Mary's execution at Fotheringay. It's time we revisited history and followed their path of destruction to the future."

THIRTY-TWO

Fotheringay Castle, England, February, Year of Our Lord 1587

Queen Mary knelt at a stark wooden prie-dieu, the small altar which provided a private sanctuary in her restricted living quarters. It was a typical piece of furniture found in the homes of the noble and privileged in this era. She knelt and prayed as she had done earlier, before the princess and Marie de Guise had made their visit. The queen was unaware of those who hovered nearby. They were almost invisible, oblivious to the others in the room. Her daughter stood at the door, the one she had relinquished at birth. The others were descendants by many generations, one being her many great grandson, King Henry. He stood in the shadowed corner with young Prince Edward and Cecil. Or, at least, it was the impression she chose to convey.

"Ladies, you may enter now," she gave a command as she pushed herself off the kneeler and stood, facing the doorway where Mary Elizabeth stood. Her eyes never reached the far corner where three figures hid in the shadows. Henry, Edward and Cecil had stood quietly, concealed, as they watched the proceedings. They watched intently the exchange between mother and daughter, who were meeting for the first time, *meeting just before the scheduled execution. Tomorrow. Early morning. Mary Queen of Scots would die at the order of her cousin, Queen Elizabeth I of England. Always the English pitted against the Scots. Would it never end?*

The queen had left her prayers and taken a seat by the fire, waving her daughter and her mother to approach. "Come here child. I have waited a lifetime in captivity for this moment."

Mary Elizabeth walked forward tentatively, curtsied and then allowed the queen to take her hand before speaking again. "You look just as I once did. So young, so beautiful, so eager and full of life. And to think you almost did not live. You were so tiny when I first held you in Loch Leven Castle. But you were there as well, were you not? You were the young lady who rescued yourself as a tiny baby, am I not right?"

"Yes, Your Majesty," Mary Elizabeth answered with respect.

"You must call me Mother," Queen Mary insisted, waving away formalities with a flutter of one hand. "For that is what I am – your mother. And, at least for tonight, we can be mother and daughter. Tomorrow they will execute me for crimes I did not commit."

"No." Mary Elizabeth couldn't stifle her groan. "I have always wanted to meet my mother. Gran, I mean Grandmother, always told me my mother was dead."

"And, I suppose you could say," Grandmother pointed out. "In the twenty-first century, your mother really was dead and for quite a few centuries at least."

Henry had to smile at the confusing connections the three were making, trying to mark one dot to the next from past to present to future and back to the past again. Time travel was such a conundrum of mixed signals and ever-changing events.

Queen Mary gave her daughter, Mary Elizabeth, a warm, fond smile. "Your grandmother always did have a way of making truths out of non-truths. It does not matter now. What matters is

I prepare you as best I can for the life you will lead. You will be queen – a queen like no other, of that I am sure."

The conversation continued to skirt the important issues and dwell on trivialities for awhile. Queen Mary put a stop to it when she handed Mary Elizabeth a document and told her to read it in old French and then to translate it into English. She was testing her daughter, but she was also making sure her daughter knew the facts. At least from her perspective.

"On this day, the 7th day of February, in the year of our Lord 1587," Mary Elizabeth read out loud the words her mother had transcribed in such neat handwriting. *"I commit myself and my faith to the Almighty and the promise of everlasting life. My dear brother, King Henry of France, brother to my sadly deceased first husband, the Dauphin Francis, who was also king before his untimely death. I beseech you to understand and know the truth of what happened. I have been tried and found guilty of treason, but my accusers have made it quite clear my fate is a result of my faith. Lord Kent told me quite bluntly, and I quote him word for word, "Your life would be the death of our religion, your death would be its life." It makes me feel stronger knowing I have upheld my faith against all odds and the general well-being of my church, the Roman Catholic Church, is dependent, to some degree, on my life."*

"Enough!" Mary Elizabeth wasn't allowed to finish. The queen startled everyone. *"This letter will be sent to the King of France. There are others. You may read them all and learn from them. There are some in Latin."* The queen then commiserated, partially confessing her faults. *"I was too proud, too determined to be the ever dominant and powerful ruler. It is not a position of luxury, my child."* The letter was placed in a casket, a treasure box for private letters, and handed to Mary Elizabeth for safe-keeping.

The casket. Henry jogged his memory. *Yes, it was still in the* secret hiding place in his chambers. Placed there before his time, by none other than the Mary Elizabeth who received it from her mother, Queen Mary. The secret hiding place was behind a large stone which was a part of the fireplace. He must look at it. There must be something in the casket, the treasure box, of significance. Otherwise, why was he hearing about it now? After so many years with no reference being made to it?

"Take this." Mary Elizabeth accepted the casket and held it with due reverence, listening intently to her mother's instructions. "Read it all and keep it safe until the letters are delivered as they should be. And remember to rule with you head and not your heart. Although your heart should reach out to your subjects. At all cost, put them and their well-being before your own."

The queen had reluctantly ended the visit. "You must go. I must prepare myself to meet my Creator. And you must be far enough away when the sword falls to ensure no one can imprison you for life as they did to me." The conversation finished. Mary Elizabeth and Marie de Guise made their exits, hugs and tears quickly exchanged. There was noise from the halls and guards crashed into the queen's chambers. Only to find her, once again, kneeling at the small altar. They didn't look in the shadows in the corner. They didn't see Henry and his companions. Not finding what they expected, the guards left as loudly as they had entered.

"I have been expecting you." She waved the men forward, away from the shadowed corner. Henry, Edward and Cecil took several steps into the room, Henry at the fore, excited to meet his many great grandmother in person. "There are evil powers at work. Both today and well into the future. I have seen the future try to destroy me and what is mine. It's all in the casket letters. You know where they are. You must read them. And you must follow the advice I have given, dictated to me from one of my descendants from the future, Queen Mary Elizabeth II. From the *twenty-fifth century." Her eyes caught Henry's in a chilling look. "Read. Find the evil. And destroy this evil. Your life, King Henry I of Scotland, many great grandson of mine, depends on it." She obviously knew who they were and why they were here. "As do the lives of your heirs, and all the rulers in Scotland's future. Now go."*

THIRTY-THREE

Holyrood House, Edinburgh, Winter, Year of Our Lord 1877

"What are you doing, Father?" Edward's voice had an edge of concern to it, not something one would expect in someone so young. "We have to move on. We can't stay here."

"I need to retrieve something, Edward. If it's still where it should be. It's an important part of our ancestral history." Henry talked rapidly as he made his way to the fireplace. He found the stone and gripped it firmly, tugging it out of its chasm. "The history of your time traveling ancestors." He reached inside and pulled out the journals, one by one. "Your Grandmother Marie's journal." He handed it to Edward. "Your Grandmother Mary Elizabeth's journal." He lay it on top of the other journal the boy held. "And so much more."

"Do you have a journal, Father?" Edward asked.

"Yes." Henry pulled out a few more journals and some paperwork. He carried it all over to his writing desk. He put down the retrieved documents and pulled a tab on the desk. An opening appeared. He reached inside and pulled out his own journal. It showed the crinkles of time, well used over the years. Sadly, it was not as concise and full of detail as the others. He would have to remedy his writing habits. He held it up for Edward to see, then tucked it back in the secret compartment of the desk. "It's safe in there for now." He walked back to the fireplace and reached his arm into the opening, deeper this time. His fingers fumbled, feeling around until he found it. Queen Mary's casket, a cache full of letters. He grasped it and juggled it carefully to bring it forward, towards him, and then through the opening.

"Queen Mary's casket," he held it up for Edward to see. "The one she mentioned. The one she gave to Grandmother Mary Elizabeth."

"Why is it so important?" Edward was just as curious as his father.

"I don't know. But I think we need to find out." He nodded at the journals still resting in Edward's hands as well as the one stacked on the desk. "Put the journals and papers back in the secret compartment for now and replace the stone securely. Just in case our little bit of research is interrupted. We don't want our hiding niche discovered."

It only took mere minutes to open the casket. Age and the elements had wreaked a certain amount of havoc on what had once been a fine piece of metalwork. Edward had returned to his side as the lock snapped and Henry lifted the lid. The hinges snapped in the process and the lid disconnected totally. Setting it aside, Henry pondered the contents. It was full of neatly folded sheets of parchment, all securely folded with the official wax seal of Mary Queen of Scots, her handwriting evident on the outer folds, identifying the person for whom the contents were addressed. On top was a letter addressed to her cousin, Henry I, Prince of Joinville, Duke of Guise, Count of Eu. Henry picked it up carefully and held it for Edward to see.

"He died just over a year after Queen Mary was executed." Henry placed the letter carefully on the desk. The seal was still in place, but was obviously loosening its hold. "Chances are, even if he had received this letter, there wasn't anything he could have done with the contents. He was quite the revolutionary himself. Did you know that?" Edward shook his head. "He founded the Catholic League in 1576 to prevent the Huguenot heir, King Henry of Navarre, from succeeding to the French throne and he was a strong adversary of France's Queen Mother, Catherine de' Medici. King Henry III had him assassinated."

He picked up a letter opener and carefully slid it under the seal, which lifted with ease. "Let's see if Queen Mary had anything to say in this letter which might help us."

Cecil, who had been standing by the door keeping watch, quickly bolted it before rushing over the to king and prince. "We have to leave. Now. Someone comes. And I don't believe they'll be friendly. Gather the letters. Leave the casket. Let's make haste."

Henry was picking up the stack of letters as Cecil talked. He tucked them carefully inside his jacket. He stood to follow Cecil and his son, stopping when a glimmer of something sparkled from the bottom of the casket captured his attention. He picked it up and, barely looking at it, shoved it in his pocket as well.

Cecil had moved towards the hidden passage. He was definitely a descendant as only Royal Stuarts knew of its existence. He ushered them inside, pulling the door closed just as heavy banging forced open the door to Henry's chambers with a resounding crash.

"He's here. Somewhere." The voice was gruff. Curt. To the point.

"The secret passageway perhaps." Another voice. Another descendant. Who else knew of the Stuart secrets? "Over here."

Cecil tugged Henry's arm with one hand, his other firmly

grasping Edward's. The king blinked and found himself in Grandmother Marie's study in the twenty-first century.

"You're here. At last." Marie greeted them. "We don't have much time. Do you have the letters?" Henry nodded. "And the jewel?" He nodded again, patting his chest to indicate they were safely tucked away. "Good. You must leave. Immediately. Mary Elizabeth. Go meet your cousins. You have a long overdue assignment from your mother."

"And you too, Grandmother?" Mary Elizabeth challenged the command. "You must come, too. You haven't seen your family in years. You must come."

Grandmother Marie gave her granddaughter a sad smile. "I think seeing their long-believed-to-be-dead cousin, the once Scottish queen and regent, would unsettle them to no end. They might even order us to be burned as witches. No. I cannot go this time. But you must. Now. Before it's too late. I will see you all in the future."

THIRTY-FOUR

Castle of Guise, Northern France, Summer, 1587

"What?" a gruff voice exclaimed in the old French spoken in noble circles in the region of Lorraine. A man sat by the fireplace, the hearth burning low, projecting little heat. Robed in the scarlet tunic of a Cardinal of the Roman Catholic Church, Henry knew instantly who the man was. Louis II, Cardinal of Guise, third son of Marie de Guise's brother, Francis, Duke of Guise.

"Who goes there?" the voice cackled, as if they man had been roughly shaken out of a deep slumber.

"Your Lordship. Cousin. It is I. Princess Mary Elizabeth, daughter of the late Queen Mary of Scotland." Mary Elizabeth stepped forward. She knelt before the man, taking his raised right hand to kiss the ecclesiastical ring. She wasn't Catholic, but she was familiar with the protocol of the era. In order to gain his respect and attention, she had to earn it. As would the others when they were introduced. "I have come with letters from Mother. Letters for you."

The older man grunted to clear his throat. "My cousin didn't have a daughter. Least of all one who lived."

"But she did and I am living proof."

"*Come closer, child.*" He squinted as Mary Elizabeth approached. "*But no longer a child, I see. Yes, you look like her. Perhaps you are her daughter.*" He reached out his hand. "*Give me the letters, then. Let's see what she has to say about all this.*" He eyes took in the people standing behind Mary Elizabeth. "*And who are all these other people who have invaded my quiet time?*"

"*More cousins, your Lordship.*"

"*Humph! Just what I need! More cousins! And they all want something from me.*" Mary Elizabeth handed him the top letter. He hesitated briefly, expecting her to pass over the lot all at once. When she didn't, he took the one offered and studied the seal intently, his eyes squinting in the process. Nodded with satisfaction. "*It is hers.*" He slipped a knife under the seal and broke it, opening the parchment paper. He sat quietly as he read.

He reached out his hand. "*The others,*" he demanded.

Mary Elizabeth paused. "*But what does it say, your Lordship?*"

"*For my eyes only.*" He snapped his fingers, impatience evident. "*The others. Now. I might have something to share after I have read them all.*"

Mary Elizabeth reluctantly handed them over. He repeated the process: studied the seal, nodded with satisfaction, slipped the knife under the seal to break it, opened the paper and quietly read. Each one in turn, starting with the one on the top and making his way to the bottom. There were six letters in all. Henry and the others remained standing at the far end of the room. No one spoke. The room was eerily quiet, except for the gentle crackling of the fire in the hearth. Even those embers were slowly dissipating as the fire burned out.

Finally, with a deep sigh, the aging cardinal re-folded the last letter and placed it on top of the others which now sat on his side table. He didn't speak immediately, allowing the silence to penetrate deeper. It was a shock when he finally did speak. "There are evil forces at play." He sounded like he was giving a homily from the pulpit to a dedicated following of churchgoers. He allowed his eyes to roam around the room, studying each person with analytical precision. "Come closer and sit," he motioned with his hands.

Henry led the way. Edward and Cecil followed. Mary Elizabeth introduced each one as they made their display of respect, kneeling and kissing his ring. The group made themselves as comfortable as possible, Mary Elizabeth, Henry and Cecil pulling up chairs and Edward sitting cross-legged on the floor. They sat in silence, allowing the cardinal to take the lead in the conversation.

"We have much to discuss."

Finally, "And who did you say this lad was?"

Mary Elizabeth explained, in greater detail than she had in her introductions, the family tree which lead to Edward's position as prince of Scotland, obviously deciding right on the spot to provide full disclosure. "I did say they were all cousins, your Lordship. And they are. Cousins from the future." She raised a hand towards Henry. "This is my many great-grandson, King Henry I of Scotland, in the year of our Lord, 1877. The boy is his son, Prince Edward, heir to the throne of Scotland. And this," she motioned towards Cecil, "is another many, many great grandson, Cecil Stuart, from the year of our Lord 2445."

Louis quickly crossed himself. "Oh my!" He whispered something which sounded like a Latin prayer and crossed himself again. "We do have evil forces in our presence." He sat forward as if he were to call out for help, but Mary Elizabeth stopped him.

"Hear us out first, Cousin. Calling your guards will not stop what is already happening. Yes, we are time travelers, a magic from the twenty-fifth century that is plaguing our history even as we speak. And we must stop it!" She paused, watching her cousin intently. When he settled back with a nod, she continued.

"We are not the evil forces, but there are evil forces which have managed to steal this ability to jump through time and they are the ones we should fear." The cardinal nodded again and waved a hand for her to continue. *"My grandmother, Marie de Guise, your father's sister, is a time traveler. It was she who rescued me from death at birth and took me to the future where they could save me. She brought me up in the twenty-first century and it was only recently I discovered my ability to jump through time. My purpose was, or I should say is, to save Scotland from being amalgamated to England when Elizabeth dies and leaves the throne to my brother, King James VI."* She paused again and studied her cousin intently. *"I will succeed, Cousin. My descendants here are living proof that I do succeed. But there are forces threatening Scottish independence throughout the centuries following my rule. It must be stopped, in the future, in the present and in the past. I have seen these evil forces. So, have the others here."*

"What is you need from me? All my niece advises is to help you. But how can I help something I don't even understand?" He shook his head, obviously befuddled. *"I can offer you blessings and prayers, but somehow I think it won't help much with the evil you describe."*

All Mary Elizabeth could do was smile. It was Henry who answered. *"We have reason to believe you have something which will help us in the battle we are now facing. Something my many great grandmother, Marie de Guise, gave to her brother and was hopefully passed down to you."*

Louis sat quietly for a few minutes, pondering, his eyes downcast as if he were studying his hands. *"The sword perhaps?"* He caught Henry's eyes with his.

"Excalibur?" Henry didn't believe in the myths, but King Arthur's sword was legendary, even in Scotland.

"Not quite." The cardinal didn't hide his smile, though it appeared more like a grimace than a smile. *"Scotland, I believe*

you must know, has its own legends, myths and magic." Henry nodded. *"The sword I speak of is the sword of King Robert the Bruce, your first Scottish king who fought for independence from the English."*

"King Robert's sword?" Henry quirked his eyebrows to emphasize his query. *"But I thought it was in safe keeping at Clackmannan Tower."* This was a five-storey tall tower at the top of King's Seat Hill in Clackmannan, not far from Stirling. Built in the fourteenth century, the tower symbolized Scottish independence due to its close association with Robert Bruce who purchased it from his cousin, the then King David II of Scotland. So much Scottish history. So much myth and legends. King Robert's sword was significant, believed to have magical powers attached to it and to whomever held it in battle. Henry wasn't convinced he believed any of this magic stuff. Then again, who was he to talk? He was merely a time traveler, living the life upon which legends and myths were built.

"My aunt, Marie de Guise, had it hidden here at the same time she sent her daughter, an infant, to the court of France. It has been in my family's safekeeping ever since. No one has asked for it. No one seems to realize it's missing."

The cardinal rose from his seat and moved slowly towards the fireplace. He reached just above the hearth and pulled out a stone. An entire row of stones pivoted outwards, revealing a long, narrow hidden compartment. He reached in with both hands and pulled out a long object. The sword. Turning carefully, he presented the sword to Henry.

"I believe this was meant for you, Your Majesty." He dipped his head in obeisance, recognizing Henry's noble rank. Henry did likewise, accepting the sword with care and respect.

He took time to study it closely, holding it reverently in his hands. Robert the Bruce, King of Scotland, was a famous warrior in Scottish history, one of the first to successfully rout the English *from their land and maintain his realm. His sword, the one Henry now held, was a symbol of his success as well as a symbol of the power of Scotland as an independent realm. Some even suggested it had such magnificent powers and the person who wielded the sword would be unstoppable, a force to be reckoned with no matter what weapons were used against him, past, present or future. It was an heroic sword. Forged of the strongest metals available in the fourteenth century, the sword was a marvel of both craftsmanship and artistry. The pommel was beautiful with the Cross of St. Andrew, patron saint of Scotland, emblazoned for all to see and for the bearer to feel the ethereal power of the saint, as he wrapped his hand firmly around the soft, black leather-bound grip held in place by a corded silver chain. The Lion of Scotland, plated in silver, marked the throat of the black leather scabbard with a rounded silver shoe at the scabbard's tip. A wide belt, the leather hardened with age and sorely in need of some oil to soften it, remained attached ready and waiting for a warrior to lay claim to its powers. Was Henry the warrior of whom legend spoke?*

Henry wrapped the belt around his waist, feeling a surge of energy and power as he did so. He slowly unsheathed the sword and held it high for the others to see. He ran a finger gingerly along its length, marveling the blade, unused for centuries, still sharp enough to do considerable damage. It even glistened in the flickering light from the fire in the hearth. The sword glistened with an electrical surge rippling from the tip to the pommel and sizzling along the king's arm.

His eyes lit up. "I am ready. For Scotland. To defend my realm."

Mary Elizabeth added the rallying battle cry of Scotland, the one she had initiated during her reign. "For now and forever."

Henry, Edward and Cecil echoed her sentiments. "For now and forever."

THIRTY-FIVE

Toronto, Summer, Year of Our Lord 2030

It was starting to feel like another home away from home. This twenty-first century mansion, as Grandmother Marie called it, was filled with marvels unheard of in the late nineteenth century. Although he never had to carry clean water to his chambers for cleaning or remove the filled containers of human waste, others took care of the task for him, it was fascinating to watch the water flow freely from a tap and to press a nob on a white enameled chair, of sorts, and watch his human waste flush away to oblivion. He had no idea where it all went, but it vanished in an instant.

Turning on a room full of lights by flicking a switch. Listening to music from a small device his son called an iPad. Watching a huge wall project images of events around the world, not all good. Edward called this magic a wide-screened TV.

He still walked around the house in a daze whenever he visited. Too much to take in with 150 years of progress and technological advances.

"Father." Henry was startled by the sound of his son's voice from behind him. It earned him a chuckle. Edward couldn't help

but notice his father's unease in such a clearly foreign setting as this. The TV was on. Loud. Edward had to shout to be heard.

"How do I turn this thing down?" Henry asked, fiddling with the little black box he was sure his son had called a remote. Remote from what, he didn't know. He kept pressing buttons and the sound projecting from the screen continued to increase substantially.

"Here." Edward took the remote from his father and showed him which button to press. "Follow the arrow. The one pointing left lowers the sound. The one pointing right increases it. And this," he pointed with his thumb, "is the on-off button." He flicked it off.

"Now may we talk?" The boy placed the remote on the table underneath the TV. They had made a jump from the France of the past to the Toronto of the future, a future well beyond Henry's lifetime. They had to regroup and make strategic plans. This was the first opportunity father and son had to talk, just the two of them.

Henry nodded and took a seat. Edward sat opposite him. "I want to see my mother." He came straight to the point. "I want to meet her. Before she dies. Before I die." Edward's mother, Isabel, had died of mysterious circumstances about a year after her incarceration at Loch Leven. It left Henry free to remarry, but he had not shown any indication or interest in sharing a throne or a bed with another woman. Trust was a big issue. Isabel had destroyed it for him. Besides, there was too much turmoil in Scotland. It wasn't a good time to start a new marriage.

Sensing his father's hesitation, Edward pushed forward to defend his request. "I understand what she did, Father. But she is still my mother."

Henry didn't say anything. He sat, studying his son intently. It was Grandmother Mary Elizabeth who broke the silence. She had entered the room and was standing by the doorway. "He has a right to visit his mother, Henry."

Henry nodded. The thought of his late wife saddened him on so many levels. "Very well. But why now? And why the comment, before you die?"

"I won't survive this battle, Father," Edward spoke with an intensity and maturity far beyond his twelve years. "I'm a hemophiliac."

"You're a what? And why was I never informed?"

Grandmother Mary Elizabeth walked over to the boy and put an arm around his shoulders. "He's right, Henry. He won't survive. You need to take another wife. Produce another heir. A Scottish lass and a true-blooded Scottish heir this time. The hemophiliac gene came from his mother. Your cousin, Leopold, was a hemophiliac. And he died young. Others in the English royal family have been plagued with this ailment as well."

"He's in his twenties. Not that young. And, Leopold hasn't died." Henry insisted. He had forgotten about his cousin's ailment. Prince Leopold, Queen Victoria's youngest son, was a hemophiliac. He had come close to death many times, but, as far as Henry knew, Leopold was still alive. In his early twenties. Surely his son could live into his twenties and even longer.

"Right." Grandmother Marie corrected herself. "This time traveling sometimes mixes up my grasp of the timeline. He will die young, though."

"But there must be treatments in the future?" Henry argued, the pain and the reality of the situation sinking in. "And why didn't you tell me?"

"There wasn't time," Grandmother Mary Elizabeth spoke slowly and carefully. "And, yes there are treatments and he has been receiving them. He was always so well when you visited, we didn't want to spoil the visit. But these treatments, clotting factor replacement therapy, where a clotting factor concentrate is infused into the blood, is not a guarantee. The disease fights back sometimes, with inhibitors. And, for Edward, the prognosis isn't good. Plus, with all these injections, he's contracted HIV."

"HIV? What's that?"

"A disease of the twentieth-century which continues to plague the human race in the twenty-fifth century." Cecil marched into the room, obviously having heard the last part of the conversation and realising a need to contribute his medical knowledge. "HIV is an acronym for human immunodeficiency virus. It's a virus which causes AIDS and it damages the person's immune system, making it easier to get sick. There's no cure. Not really. And with Edward's system already compromised with the hemophiliac condition, it's only a matter of time."

"So, there's nothing can be done in your time either?" Henry ran his hands through his scalp, his agony at discovering his son was dying obvious.

Cecil shook his head sadly. "Unfortunately, no. If he sustains an injury, he could bleed to death. If an injury doesn't take his life, then the HIV or the AIDS will kill him in a few years."

Henry was groping to understand all these medical complications. His family had always been so healthy. Died of old age. What was this hemophiliac and now HIV and AIDS? And why was his family, his son, suddenly infected? Medicine had certainly progressed considerably over the centuries, but there was still a long way to go.

"Father," Edward's voice startled Henry from his thoughts. "Father. I want to die a hero. Like James Stuart, Grandmother Mary Elizabeth's love. It's better to go that way. Like a hero. Better than wasting away until death invades. Don't you think?"

Edward. His young son. So mature beyond his years. He would never reach adulthood. Never love and marry. Never rule the country he was destined to rule. Tragic. Unfair. He pulled his son into a fierce hug and blinked his eyes tight to prevent the tears from escaping. A couple did anyway.

"Time is a-wasting." Cecil rubbed his hands together, a nervous habit he was demonstrating more frequently as tensions rose. "If you're going to visit his mother, best to make it quick. Then we must make haste to the future. Before it's too late."

"Isn't that a bit of an oxymoron, Uncle Cecil." Edward pushed away from his father, trying to ease the burden of his news.

No one laughed. The seriousness of the boy's news and the impending doom threatening them all was too much to wash over with glib comments.

Henry nodded. "Come along, son. Let's go see your mother. We'll meet the rest of you shortly in the twenty-fifth century."

THIRTY-SIX

Loch Leven Castle, Late Spring, 1877

"You came. I knew you would come. Eventually. And who is this?" Isabel remained seated by the fire, wrapped in many layers of fur coverings to ward off the chill. Her skin had a pallor only death could beat. She released a cough and wiped her mouth with the back of her hand, a callous move speaking only of her decline in both body and spirit. She obviously no longer cared what anyone thought of her.

"Edward." Henry approached slowly, leading Edward gently with a few nudges on the arm. "Your son."

"My son is an infant. This is a young man. It can't be Edward."

"Time passes, Isabel. More quickly than you realize. This is Edward. Your son. My son."

"Is he?" She quirked an eyebrow. Henry wasn't sure if she was goading him with the ongoing nagging suspicion Edward wasn't his son. He let it pass. No point in upsetting the visit, upsetting Edward. He had so little time left to spend with his son. For it's what he was. His son. In every sense of the word. There was a bond which could only exist between father and son.

Henry wrapped one arm around his son, resting a hand on the boy's shoulder. It was a show of solidarity. A sign he claimed Edward as his son, regardless of the suspicious allegations of his ex-wife.

"Mother." Edward's voice was small, almost shallow, swallowed by the emptiness and cold chill of the room. He left his father's side and walked up to his mother, kneeling at her feet. "Mother. I wanted to meet you. Finally."

Tears dribbled down the woman's cheeks as she reached towards her son and made a fierce grab to engulf him in a hug, grasping at some thread of the past in the hopes to make amends or, at least, to restore what she once had as Queen of Scotland. She made a fast swipe of her dampened cheeks to wipe away the moisture before it was noticed. The tears kept coming. They were noticed. "Edward. My son." She sniffled. She glanced up suddenly, her eyes piercing a glare of hatred at Henry. "Some privacy, please." It was part request, part command. Henry would have none of it. How dare she think, even now, she could command him? The king.

He shook his head. "I'll sit over here. It's all the privacy you need."

She glared more intensely, but Henry shifted his eyes towards his son, ignoring hers. "Ten minutes, Edward. Then we must leave."

Isabel shrieked. "Ten minutes? It's not enough time. I haven't seen my son since he was born."

He returned his gaze to his ex-wife and forced a sad smile on his face. He was sure it was more of a grimace than a smile. "You didn't care about him then, Isabel. And I'm sure you don't care about him any more today than you did at his birth."

"That's not true!"

"You're wasting time, Isabel." He nodded at his son. "Ten minutes." Edward nodded back. He understood. Sad as it was, *this was not the mother-son reunion he had hoped for. His mother had yet to let him go, her hug becoming more of a vice grip than a motherly embrace.*

Edward squirmed and somehow loosened the grip. She relinquished him and he breathed more easily as he took a seat opposite her.

"How old are you now, Edward?" she asked.

"I just had my twelfth birthday."

"Twelve. A birthday. I didn't get you a gift."

"It's all right, Mother. Father gave me a fine bow and arrow set."

She harrumphed. "Now what would you need it for?"

"I am a good archer, Mother. And I like to shoot my arrows."

"Well. As long as it's just for recreation. You are much too young to be learning how to use weapons for battle."

"Not really, Mother. History is full of young princes fighting battles at my age. And, princes younger than me becoming king, like England's Edward VI."

"But he never fought any battles, my son. He was much too sickly. Sad, but true."

"Yes, Mother. Perhaps not the best choice for comparison. But I would rather die a hero than a sick young man."

Isabel gave her son a weak smile. "I would rather you did not die at all. You must live to claim your right as King of Scotland and then marry a fine English princess to combine the two countries. Scotland should be part of England. It really should."

"That's traitorous talk, Mother. And I don't agree. Scotland is much better off on its own. It's a proud and strong nation, full of potential and possibilities."

"Fine words for a young man mimicking his father." She shook her head sadly. "Had I been taking care of you and monitoring your upbringing, you would have thought different."

"I don't think so, Mother." Edward stood suddenly. "Our

time is up. I must go. I won't be seeing you again, Mother. Not in this world."

She reached out her hand, but Edward ignored it. He gave her a curt "Goodbye" and followed his father out the door and into another time.

THIRTY-SEVEN

Balmoral Castle, June 1st, Year of Our Lord 1861

"Uncle Harry." Two young boys greeted Edward's father enthusiastically.

"That's me." Henry pointed to the young man on the left, standing over a table covered with plans. He wanted his son to see some of his own past, his own youth. He wanted Edward to see Balmoral in its infancy. *"Just a little older than you are now. And there's Edward, Prince of Wales. We called him Bertie. We were close back then. Not so much now. Sadly."*

"And this is Balmoral?" Edward asked, his voice bearing witness to a sense of awe.

"Yes. I worked alongside Prince Albert, Queen Victoria's husband. He was a fine craftsman. A genius. I learned a lot from him." He motioned forward. *"Come. I'll introduce you."*

"Have you traveled through time yet?" Edward asked in a whisper.

"Yes. But my cousin, Bertie, thinks it's all fantasy and frequently makes fun of me and my stories about traveling through time."

Young Henry ran towards them and wrapped his arms

around the older Henry in a big hug. "Who did you bring with you this time, Uncle Harry." The two shared a wink of knowing. Young Henry obviously knew this man he called uncle was actually himself in the future.

"Henry. Meet my son, Edward."

"My son?" The young man whispered then coughed to mask his comment as the Prince of Wales approached. He quickly recovered and patted the young Prince of Wales on the back fondly. "Edward. Meet Edward." He motioned from one to the other. The two Edwards took their cue, chuckled and shook hands.

"Uncle Harry," Bertie nodded to the king. They had met before, but not in some time. And they would meet again.

"Father brought me here to meet Prince Albert and study the progress of Balmoral." Young Edward was eager to learn. While he could. While he still lived.

"Come." Young Henry led the way over to the table where the plans were spread out and Prince Albert was leaning over them, studying them closely.

"And who have we here?" the prince consort straightened and studied the three young boys.

"Another cousin," young Henry chuckled. "This is Edward."

"Another Edward?" Albert shook his head, winked at his son and added, "Just what we need. Another Edward."

"He wants to see the plans. He's interested in what we're doing."

"Well, it's something, isn't it? Come here, lad. I'll show you what we have planned on paper and then we'll all take a walk around the site."

THIRTY-EIGHT

India, November, Year of Our Lord 1875

Henry and Edward stood at the large window of the grand house, watching the events unfold below them. The guards were scrambling to secure the area as armed men fought to make an entrance. In many ways, it was no different than the Scotland they had left behind. The heat and humidity, the dress, the architecture, the décor, all suggested otherwise.

A door opened behind them and the two moved away from the window.

"Henry. Again. And this must be your son. We met many years ago at Balmoral. Amazing how little you've aged since then. Both of you." The Prince of Wales quirked an eyebrow as if expecting to be greeted with a chuckle from his unexpected guests. He was, after all, trying to be funny.

"Another battle being fought?" Henry motioned his head towards the window. "Still unable to squelch the natives?"

"You should talk, Henry." The prince, having waved away his attendants and shut the door firmly behind him, made his way to the cabinet along the far wall. He picked up a decanter and proceeded to pour some of the thick brown substance into a finely *cut crystal glass. He raised it towards Henry. "Care for a glass, Cousin?" Henry shook his head. "And what about you, young man?" Shocked, young Edward took a step back, shadowing his father's form. The prince just laughed, lifted the glass to his lips and downed the substance all in one gulp. Placing the empty vessel on the table with a clatter, he shrugged out of his jacket and tossed it over a nearby chair. He rolled up his sleeves and undid the top fasteners of his shirt, rolling his head as if to further release the pressure which had once restricted neck movement. "Ah! That's better." He poured himself another glass and made his way over to a chair close to the window where there was a minimal amount of air flow from the open window. "Confounded heat. Don't know how they stand it. I shan't be complaining about the cold damp of England when I return. It will be a blessed change from this." He dug out a handkerchief and mopped the sweat from his brow. "Now. Sit. You didn't come all this way through all of time just to talk about the balmy weather in India." He motioned to chairs opposite him and stretched out his legs to get comfortable. "Sit."*

"We're not here at your beck and call," Henry retorted, maintaining his standing pose. "And I do outrank you, Cousin Edward. So, you can stop ordering me about."

"Oh! Don't get into that." The prince was never one to mask his displeasure. And, he was obviously angry with Henry. "I've had a lifetime of watching you get what you want so easily and so quickly. Not anymore. Now what do you want?"

"Get what I want? And so easily? What do you mean by that?" Henry was better at hiding his anger. To a point. His nerves were on edge and he was showing signs of losing his patience. Not just with his cousin, but with everyone.

"You have to ask?" It was more of a question than a statement. "You were king before you came of age. Here I am, in my mid-thirties, and still just a little prince waiting for his crown.

You've had years to make a mark on your country and your people. And me?" He snorted in disgust. "Just the merry prince. That's what I am."

"And what have you done with the time?" Henry snapped. "Whored yourself to whatever skirt caught your liking?"

"Enough!" the prince bellowed, tossing the now empty glass at Henry. It missed and shattered just behind his son. "There's never been anything I could do. Nothing I was allowed to do. Until now. Here. In this miserably hot, humid climate. India. She wants to be Empress of India. Ruler of the world. And why not?" He gave a show of shrugging his shoulders, as if he didn't care. "And what does that make me?" He snorted. "Nothing more than I ever was. Just a pawn. A figurehead."

The prince shot a look at both Henry and Edward which suggested piercing daggers. It worked. Partially. Edward jumped back a step. His father stayed rooted where he stood. "I want to be king, Henry. It's all I've ever wanted. To be King of England. By the time I'm king, if I live long enough, I'll be too old to enjoy the privilege of the position of power."

Henry let out a sharp laugh. "It's not all that wonderful, Cousin. Believe me. It's not all about fine clothes, parading around in luxurious robes, hosting elaborate parties. And it can be dangerous."

Bertie laughed, slapping his hands on the arms of his chair. "Well. I guess you would know, wouldn't you? The danger, I mean. You get what you deserve in this life, I suppose."

"Which means you deserve your princedom," Henry counter-attacked. "And the danger? I have no one but the English to blame."

Anger flashed across the prince's face, a red blush spreading from his neckline up to his forehead. "Careful. I can still call the guards."

"And we'd be gone before they arrived," Henry pointed out.

"Like I said, you get what you deserve. England deserves the right to rule the world. And that includes Scotland."

"No, it doesn't!" It was young Edward's turn to demonstrate anger as cool and as sharp as ice. "Scotland has just as much right to be free and independent as any other country in this world. Including India. England may have the upper hand of its colonies now. But just wait. You're all so arrogant and bullyish. It will be your downfall. Just wait."

The English prince let out a cacophonous explosion of laughter, so intense tears leaked from the corners of his eyes. He wiped them away and pointed at Henry. "Your son has a temper and a sense of humor. An amusing combination, wouldn't you agree?"

"He's right, Cousin. And you'd do well to think on what he said. One country can't rule the entire world. Neither does it have the right to do so. Back off with Scotland."

The prince just snorted. "Or what? Are you threatening me, Cousin?"

Henry and Edward had vanished. The prince was alone. His thoughts ravaged his mind. "Typical. Always slithering to another timeline to avoid both truth and consequences. Oh well! They'll soon see who's boss." Standing up, he walked over to the side table, ignoring the crunching of broken glass as he slowly moved towards another glass of mind-numbing sustenance.

THIRTY-NINE

Secure Facility, Holyrood House, Edinburgh, Year of Our Lord 2445

"You took your time, Your Majesty," Cecil greeted Henry and Edward when they appeared in Henry's private chambers of the future.

"Edward had a couple of requests. We made a few stops along the way." He shrugged his shoulders to brush off Cecil's concerns. "We agreed to meet at this time and place and we're here now. At the agreed time and place."

Cecil nodded. "True enough, I suppose. All time is relative, is it not? Well," he rubbed his hands together. "No more time to waste. The queen awaits. Follow me."

"I think I know the way." Henry muttered, but followed along as instructed.

"Perhaps in your time. But a lot of things have changed over the centuries." Cecil led them out of the chambers, down the long corridor which had once been a gallery of masterpieces hanging on every spare space of wall. Everything was barren now, sterile. Artificial. Devoid of light, color, and, yes, life. In other words, it was dull. They followed Cecil down the back stairs, the ones once

used by staff only and along another hall leading towards the front, towards the greeting area, sometimes dubbed, at least in Henry's time, as the state room. Cecil opened the double doors and motioned them inside.

"Some things never change," Henry muttered as he studied the space, still draped with grand armor from centuries before even his time and paintings which must be worth more than a fortune in this era. In his day, there had been over a hundred portraits of Scottish royalty hanging in this room. There were many more, obviously added over the centuries. The room itself was sumptuous with elaborate plaster work ceilings and finely polished wood carvings.

Satisfied he was in a familiar space, he glanced at the alcove and the grand chairs, the pair of thrones, which had held a place of honor since the days of King David I who sighted a vision of a stag with a glowing cross between its antlers and built an abbey on the site which later became the Palace of Holyrood, or Holy Cross. Seated on one of the thrones was a woman Henry didn't recognize, though her features were surprisingly familiar. Two other women stood nearby, conversing. Henry recognized them immediately: Grandmother Marie and Grandmother Mary Elizabeth. Everyone paused in their conversation, taking notice of Henry and Edward's entrance. Cecil walked briskly forward and bowed to the woman seated on the throne.

"Your Majesty," he spoke clear and with distinction. "May I present His Majesty, King Henry I and his son, Prince Edward." Turning to Henry, he added, "Your Majesty, this is Her Majesty, Queen Mary Elizabeth II, Queen of Scotland in the twenty-fifth century."

The current queen stood and walked towards the men, hand extended. She chuckled softly. "Since we're all kings, queens and princes, here, we won't stand on ceremony. There is work to be done. A pleasure to meet you at last, Henry. And you too, young

Edward." She nodded to the boy. She pointed to the chairs near the window. "Sit. Please. I'm sure you have lots of questions. I'll answer them as best I can."

"I do have lots of questions," Henry admitted, waiting for the women to be seated before taking a seat himself. "But I don't know where to begin."

"I do," Edward chirped in. The others chuckled at his boldness. "How did this time travel anomaly begin?"

"That's a big question, Edward," Queen Mary Elizabeth II answered. "But a good one. Cecil?" She shared a knowing nod with the man. "He's the man to outline the program's beginnings. After all, he was the one to invent and implement it."

"Cecil?" Four sets of eyes flickered suddenly to the man, watching him shift uncomfortably.

"You've been holding out on us," Henry spoke for the others. "I guess you have some explaining to do."

A deep sigh escaped Cecil as he took time to gather his thoughts before speaking. "Yes. I did invent the implant time travel device," he finally admitted. He motioned to someone standing by the door to bring over a large board. Once it was wheeled into place, he lifted a large page and threw it over the back, revealing a huge image of what appeared to be the human brain. "We may be far advanced in many ways, but sometimes the old-fashioned way of showing diagrams works best."

"And it's more secure," the queen added.

Cecil nodded, picked up a pointer and proceeded with his presentation. "Now, back to the project. I wasn't alone in the research and development. It did get out of control and files went missing. We know now where the files disappeared. To a similar research lab just outside of London. The idea of the implant, once I had tested it, was to choose subjects to carry out specific tasks in the past, to change a little bit of history, to make things better in the present day of the twenty-fifth century. Especially for Scotland and the Scottish people. It wasn't my idea to erase your memories of each visit to this place well in your future." He cast an accusing eye at the queen.

"I was advised on this matter, Cecil," she argued in her defense. "You know that. We didn't want our chosen subjects to know too much, to be able to access this secure facility without our knowledge or our control. Especially since the implant monitored brain activity and manipulated the jump through time based on what, where and when the person was thinking about."

Cecil cleared his throat, fiddling with the pointer in his hand. "Be that as it may, it obviously didn't work on everyone. Henry, here, is perhaps the first of our subjects, that we know of, whose memory was never fully erased. He has a strong mind, that one. As does his son, Edward." The boy beamed at the praise.

"The implant works on navigating specific parts of the brain." He started pointing at the diagram of the human brain, paying specific attention to various areas, each labeled with an identifying name. He didn't go into detail about each part. Instead, he summarized as best he could. He knew the importance of making things brief, especially when expediency was an essential factor. "Since the brain is basically made up of nerve cells which interact with the rest of the body through the spinal cord and nervous system, the positioning of the implant is crucial to its effectiveness. It is surgically placed between the brain stem, which basically controls all functions of the body, and the spinal cord." He used the pointer again and marked a specific location on the diagram. "Here," he said. "It's most effective here. Tiny wires, replicating the nerve cells which relay messages from various parts of the brain to the rest of the body, project from this implant, making it function much like any other part of the brain, but also along with all the various brain parts." He paused, noting the looks of confusion on the faces listening to his explanation. "Simply put, as my queen just explained, all you have to do is think of a time and place and the implant opens a wormhole allowing you to move to that time and place." He placed the pointer on the ledge at the bottom of the board and returned to his seat. It appeared he fully expected questions. A lot of questions. There were none.

Queen Mary Elizabeth II allowed the details to sink in for a few minutes before taking over the discussion. "We were careful who we chose," she paused, allowing the impact of her confession to settle in. "Our sole purpose was to make sure Scotland remained free and independent. We were faced with a crisis in this time. England was gaining power, partly through stealing our time travel technology. But it was more than that. They wanted what we had found centuries ago in the northern seas: oil. By international law, the waters around Scotland belong to Scotland. If Scotland amalgamated with England..."

"Or was overrun by the English," Cecil grumpily interrupted. He didn't say any more, noticing his sovereign's raised hand as an indication he had overstepped his rights. She had the floor. It was her place to say what he was thinking. It was not uncommon for one to finish the other's sentences, but this was neither the time nor the place.

The queen concluded the obvious, "Then England would have the rights to whatever came out of the northern seas. Including the oil. We have been fighting this battle for a long time and, with Cecil's invention, we thought we had the upper hand. Then somehow the English managed to create their own implant-time travel program and started sending soldiers through wormholes to all times and places, wreaking havoc for generations of Scottish people, particularly those they somehow knew had the implants imbedded in their skulls."

"So how can we help?" Henry asked the obvious. "We don't have the weapons of your time. We don't have the means to defeat them now or in the past."

"But your minds are simpler than theirs." She held up her hand to ward off argument. *"No insult intended. It's actually a bonus. They can't read your minds as well as they can read the minds of this century. They can't sense your presence. You have the ability to become almost invisible while infiltrating their facilities. And, with Cecil's help, we can make you completely invisible."*

"You have the technology?" Edward asked. Cecil nodded. *"Cool."*

"Cool? What do you mean?" Henry asked. *"You're not cold, are you son?"*

Everyone laughed. *"What's so funny?"* The king's eyes took in the sea of amused faces. *"He said he was cold. That can't be good."*

"It's a socially acceptable slang word of the twentieth and twenty-first centuries," Grandmother Marie explained. *"It took me a while to catch on when the younger Mary Elizabeth started using it."*

"It means everything's great. Awesome. Fantastic." Grandmother Mary Elizabeth added a definition of sorts. *"In this case, I think Edward is impressed with the idea of becoming invisible."*

"Very cool." Edward nodded in agreement. The others laughed some more.

Cecil cleared his throat to regain everyone's attention. *"We have a few things we need to do with your implants before you're ready to send into the field, so to speak."*

"And, we want to train you on some of our newest high-tech weapons before you leave," the queen added.

"Cool!" Edward said. *"Can I bring my bow and arrows as well?"*

"Wouldn't hurt," Henry ruffled his son's hair affectionately, until the boy squirmed out of his reach. He cleared his throat softly to mask a chuckle. His son was growing up. All too fast.

The memory of his son's confession about the disease sparked its worrying head, but the king squelched it back down. Time to mourn later. Now was a time for action.

The queen added, "And, Henry, you must bring the sword. King Robert's sword. That, and the ring, are connected. Powerful. In ways you will never begin to understand."

"Was he a time traveler, too?" Edward asked, eager to know more than just his history. He wanted to know all he could about the time travelers, past, present and future.

"Yes, he was," Cecil gave the lad an affectionate smile. He showed a fondness one would expect between a father and son, not a young boy and a distant descendant. "He was the first. Our first. He wore the ring your father now wears. The ring Grandmother Mary Elizabeth still wears as she hasn't finished her journey through life, past, present and future. He also wielded the great sword that is now in your father's possession, the one we retrieved from Grandmother Marie's cousin, Louis II, Cardinal of Guise."

Looking around the group, he suggested, "We have some time, I believe for some questions." He received a nod of agreement from the queen.

FORTY

"Why were we chosen?" Grandmother Marie asked the most obvious question which was at the forefront of all their minds.

"There were others." Queen Mary Elizabeth II took the floor. "Not always royalty. Some survived, but were ineffective. They were the pawns in a much larger experiment. You have to understand. This program was seen as a means to protect Scotland as a free and independent country throughout the centuries. When we first started, we, the Scottish people, were British subjects, along with the Irish and so many other people around the world. We studied Scotland's history and decided to pinpoint key characters in the long battle for Scottish supremacy. Our studies first took us back as far as King Robert I or Robert the Bruce. In our original timeline, which had me as a mere Royal Stuart of no consequence under English rule, our independence was lost in the Battle of Bannockburn in 1314. The thirteenth and fourteenth centuries were a continuous series of battles between England and Scotland. King Edward I of England was successful multiple times, conquering most of Scotland. Robert always fought back, valiantly regaining control in 1314, first at Stirling, still our most strategic battle site. After King Edward II was crowned King of

England, he fought back, gaining ground until Bannockburn. It was a tough battle, the English losing ground on all sides. In the original timeline, Robert was killed and the Scots lost to the English, who maintained their control of Scotland right up to our era. It wasn't a pleasant marriage, if you can call it that. We had to change the timeline. We chose to start our venture with King Robert."

Cecil took over the discourse. "We made Robert our first royal time traveler and helped him regain what was rightfully ours."

"And we managed to hold onto our land," Queen Mary Elizabeth II took over again. "Until your era." She paused to look at Grandmother Marie. "You had a difficult task, Marie de Guise. You managed to keep the English at bay, so to speak. But it wasn't easy. We helped as best we could, keeping our presence and your implant and time travel abilities as secret and inconsequential as possible. Your daughter was not a good subject to enlist in this program. Your granddaughter, however. We knew we had a chance there if we put you, as the loving grandmother and a seasoned time traveler, beside her as a guide."

Grandmother Marie interrupted. "I never did fully understand how it was possible for an infant to jump through time. She didn't have her implant until much later."

Henry sat up straight, a sudden realisation invading his senses. "Nor did Edward. And he jumped through time, nestled as a baby in my arms."

Grandmother Marie added another point which she never fully understood. "And how does my cousin and close confidante, Lady Mary Catherine de Guise, fit into all this? She was neither royal nor a key player in Scottish affairs."

The queen held up her hands to ward off further questions until she had answered those already presented. "We specifically chose Lady Mary Catherine, knowing full well how close she was to you. We knew you would need someone familiar and under-standing by your side. Yours was the most difficult journey to take. As for the babies? We didn't know if it would work either until Lady Mary Catherine managed to secret the infant Princess Mary Elizabeth to the future. Then Henry was able to do the same with his son." She nodded at Cecil to take over.

"We haven't fully studied the matter yet," he explained quite simply. "Too many other matters, more serious matters, to contend with. However, it appears the implant provides an aura around the person, enough to encompass what a person's wear-ing, any jewels or weapons or documents they're carrying and, yes, something as tiny as a newborn baby."

"But there were others." Grandmother Marie continued to argue. "Lady Mary Catherine mentioned others she knew amongst the clans. People who were time travelers."

"All dedicated to the cause of Scottish independence," the queen concluded for her ancestor. Grandmother Marie nodded. "The cause was our main intent. Our goal. Our initiative. But now things have gotten somewhat out of hand and we need your help to eliminate the English time travelers' ability to wreak havoc in our plans."

"Do you have a mole amongst you?" Edward asked. "A spy? A double agent?"

The queen nodded sadly. "Quite possibly. We believe we know who. There are several. We don't want to let them know what we know until we complete our mission. For the moment, they're a means of feeding false intel to the enemy."

"Suffice it to say," Cecil added. "It is imperative we only talk freely in this room, which is the only safe room in the realm." He waved off further questions. "We have created a state-of-the-art facility here at Holyrood House, but only this room is truly safe. It's only accessible to certain people and there are multiple layers of cyber walls around us to protect anything said or discussed in this room." He stood and motioned the others to follow. "That being said, we are about to enter a room which serves to monitor all of our time travelers and many of England's as well. Be careful what you say outside this room."

Cecil opened the door which led to what the others remembered as being the formal dining room. The walls were covered in large screens projecting images of various events, presumabyle around Scotland and throughout time. The long dining table which had once hosted dignitaries from around the world was covered with unfamiliar devices imitating the keyboard of a typewriter. People were seated before these devices, typing feverishly.

Henry had seen typewriters. In fact, he owned several and often typed formal letters on the machine before adding his official signature. The typewriter was, after all, a Scottish invention, though the English often tried to claim it as their own. A Henry Mill created a device in 1714, but a Lawrence Murray had created a much better device ten year's earlier. Another bone of contention for the English was the Scottish collaboration with the American inventor, Franz Wagner, to produce a keyboard layout which would assist typists to type without looking at the keyboard. An ingenious design.

These devices, however, were nothing like the typewriters of his time. Lying flat on the table, the layout of the letters on a keyboard was similar, but the similarities ended there.

"Computers, Father," Edward whispered in Henry's ear. Something else his son understood better than he did, having been educated in the twenty-first century. "They control everything."

Edward, never shy, moved ahead of the others who remained by the door gawking at the setup. He wandered around, taking in all the devices. "It's like a superhero cave!" Edward exclaimed with delight.

Cecil laughed. The others weren't too sure. "A superhero cave?" Henry quirked an eyebrow.

"Yeah. A cave with all kinds of high-tech stuff that helps superheroes fight evil."

Henry nodded his head. "Right." He rubbed his chin thoughtfully. "What exactly is happening here, Cecil?"

"Quite simply, we're monitoring the implants."

"In other words, spying on your experimental subjects," Grandmother Marie pointed out.

"Another way of looking at it." Cecil nodded. "Yes. It's our way of controlling what happens. If things look like they might be getting out of hand, so to speak, we can send in reinforcements, or pull the subject out of the situation they find themselves in. Like when Henry was cornered in the nursery cubbyhole with his infant son."

"You provided a means to escape to another time and place," Henry concluded.

"And when you, Marie, along with your granddaughter and your faithful servant, were cornered in your study in Toronto."

"In other words, you always had our backs," Henry noted with a satisfied nod of his head.

"In a manner of speaking and as best we could." Cecil motioned everyone forward. "We watch your progress on monitors. Nothing private, rest assured. We allow you some sense of privacy. We don't interfere unless there appears to be no other alternative."

"So, you play God," Grandmother Mary Elizabeth was never one to mince words. She always came straight to the point. "You have the upper hand, controlling all of us and the outcome of our affairs. Making sure that what we will do will positively affect your world in your time."

"A blunt way of putting it," Cecil agreed. "But you also played God. You jumped around at will to make sure things were going the way you believed they should. Your jumps to visit Queen Elizabeth I of England, your brother, your mother and father. Those jumps were neither planned nor controlled by us at this end. You had your own list of ulterior motives."

"Perhaps we all play God at times," Queen Mary Elizabeth II suggested. She waved a hand towards the empty chairs around the table. "Please. Take a seat. We still have much to discuss. A lot to explain."

FORTY-ONE

Stirling Castle, Year of Our Lord 1314

*"I have been expecting you, many great grandson of mine."
The man standing at the hearth waved Henry forward. "Come.
Warm yourself by the fire. It has been a cold, damp day. But we
did well. I had the support I needed, so thank those from the
future. We are free of the English plague. For now."*

"No need to thank those of the future," Henry replied calmly
as he made his way towards this great king. Robert the Bruce was
a legendary figure in Scottish history. Henry would know him
anywhere. It was fitting he should visit him now. On the night
before his own great battle with the English. Well into the future.
"They watch our every move."

*Robert laughed. A deep, hearty laugh. "Aye and I am sure
they do. I know I would if I had the means they have. What a
wonderful world the future time. Would I could live long enough
to see it."*

"Oh. They have their problems, too."

*Henry now stood close to his ancestor. What happened next
was both sudden and unexpected. Robert set down the cup he*

was holding and pulled Henry into a warm embrace, patting him fondly on the back as if he were a long-lost friend. The fourteenth century king placed his hands on Henry's shoulders, gripping firmly and holding him at arm's length to study him further. Satisfied, he let go with a nod. "Yes," he said. "You are my descendant." He made his way to a sturdy, wooden chair, intricately carved, and sat down, waving Henry to do the same in the chair facing him.

"We have much discuss," Robert raised a cup. "Would you care for some cider?" Henry shook his head and watched the great king of old as he took a big mouthful and swallowed. Satisfied, he placed the cup on the table next to him and pondered his next words before speaking. "I understand you are the one who will carry my sword. Raised it many times, I have, against those scoundrels from the south. Glad to report that they all fled in many directions each time I raised it. Unfortunately, those English never give up. They just do not seem to understand. Scotland is ours. Not theirs."

"I have the sword." Henry watched his ancestor intently. "It was held in safekeeping for centuries."

"Marie de Guise and her extensive French family." Robert took another sip of cider, this time continuing to hold his cup with both hands as he pulled his lips together tightly as if to compress any remnants of the liquid into his mouth, not to be wasted. Noticing Henry's raised eyebrow, he chuckled softly. "Yes, I have met the woman herself. As well as her granddaughter. Mary Elizabeth. A good queen in her time. She didn't need the sword. But I fear you do."

Henry nodded. "It has some powers, I am led to believe. But possessing a more scientific mind, I am rather skeptical."

"Understandable." Robert paused, garnering his thoughts before saying more. "We may have won the battle today, the

battle of Bannockburn, as I believe they will call it in the future. But the war with our southern neighbors is far from over. And they have a new weapon at their beck and call, it would seem. A weapon of manpower and weapons the like we have never seen. At least not in my time. Perhaps not in yours either. You must wipe them out in the future, Henry. Wipe them out so they can't interfere with our lives. Scotland wants to heal and prosper. And it will. In my time. In Mary Elizabeth's time. And in your time. But it might not have a chance if these future powers take over the past, my present."

Henry nodded in both understanding and agreement. "What do I need to know about this sword?"

Robert quickly downed the rest of the contents of his cup and placed it on the side table. He pushed himself from his seat and walked over to the table under the row of lead-pained windows. He picked up the sword. His sword. The same one Henry had strapped to his side. Only Henry's was centuries older. Robert pulled the sword from its scabbard and faced Henry.

Holding it up high, in front of his face, he studied the weapon from its sharp tip to the pommel at the opposite end of the grip. "Magnificent. Isn't it?" He glanced across to Henry who had also stood up, pulling his sword, Robert's sword, from the scabbard and held it before him, mimicking his ancestor's pose. "I see you have my sword," Robert exclaimed. "It's showing its age, but still as magnificent as ever. Don't you agree?" Henry nodded. "Shall we?" Without waiting, Robert allowed his sword to lie forward as the man who gripped it, commanded, "On guard."

It was as if the sword had a mind of its own. Henry felt his arm being pulled and tugged in every direction as he warded off blow after blow. His opponent's sword copied, mimicked. As it should, since it was one and the same sword.

"You cannot lose with this sword in your hand, Henry,"

Robert called out as the two continued to parry. "It has a mind and a power of its own. Believe in it. But never let it go. Never allow anyone else to handle it at any time. The power is within you and within the sword. You are now connected to each other." He was still talking but the sound of his voice was fading. As was Henry. "Believe, Henry. For now and forever. Believe."

FORTY-TWO

Buckingham Palace, London, Year of Our Lord 2445

"Father," Edward whispered as the two time travelers hovered in a dark corner, waiting Cecil's signal. "If we manage to destroy all the implants, how do we return to our time? And, how can we be sure someone else won't invent something similar and use it for their evil purposes?"

Henry wondered the same thing, but he had no answers for his son. His mind was focussed only on the current task at hand. "You'll have to ask Cecil, son." He couldn't think of any other way to respond.

Cecil's return, with a stern shush warning, prevented further discussion. "The grandmothers are ensconced at the far end of the hall. They'll stay hidden until our signal." The man spoke in barely more than a whisper. His instructions were unnecessary as they had already gone over the plans in great detail. Many times.

Cecil would lead Henry and Cecil into the audience chamber, or what had been the audience chamber on the main floor of the grand palace. The men were hidden around the corner off the Marble Hall staircase; the women in a staircase at the opposite end of the hall. The women's job was to prevent others from accessing the floor around the audience chamber once the action started. They would also set off some explosives at random locations throughout the main floor to divert attention from the main attack in the audience chamber, the English ground zero of time travel.

Cecil had explained how the audience chamber, complete with its fine furnishings, including the concert grand piano, had long since been cleared away to facilitate the production and monitoring of the time travelers. It was in effect their war room, the place where they planned all military exercises throughout time. Cecil would use his handheld implant monitor to adjust their body chemistry and make them invisible, until such time as they were in the room and able to disable much of the system. Once the women received the 'all clear' signal and they had set off the diverting explosives, they would make their way down into the lower regions of the palace where the English soldiers were implanted and trained. The queens had special devices, developed by Cecil, to disengage every implant which had been installed and destroy the implants waiting to be inserted. They knew the English soldiers currently in the implant region were already sedated. Cecil had managed to secure the necessary intel to time this operation at a crucial point in the implanting of new soldiers.

The Scottish warriors of the past and present each had their weapons of choice, as well as the weapons of the century, designed by none other than Cecil.

"Ready?" Cecil asked. Henry and Edward nodded in unison. They were the only ones forging this part of the battle. They were the only ones with the capabilities of becoming invisible and wreaking the most havoc. "Let's do it, then. Buckingham Palace will never be the same once we're done." He fiddled with a device on his wrist, then paused briefly to add, "Don't forget to follow our plan completely. Once I press this button, we shall be invisi-

ble. Completely. Even to ourselves." He tapped the button and whispered the final command, "Let's go."

Henry glanced around him. He couldn't see his son. He couldn't see Cecil. He couldn't hear them, other than a faint whisper of a breath here and there. Even their footsteps were muffled, as Cecil had insisted they wear cloth coverings on their shoes. He didn't want them running around in sock feet, in case they had to make a speedy exit through the gardens. It wouldn't do the feet any good to be battered and bruised by stones and other sharp objects piercing through the socks. He had provided what he called surgical booties to cover the shoes and muffle the sound. As long as they didn't move quickly and stomp their feet, the muffling worked like a charm. Should a fast escape be required, the friction of fast-moving feet on the ground was enough to rip off the booties.

A door whooshed open and someone stepped out. Before it could close, Henry slid into the audience chamber, a.k.a. the war room. He assumed the others had done likewise. He moved around the room to get into position, being careful not to jostle the men and women at the consoles and other equipment which beeped and projected images from across the time warp. It was much like the setup at Holyrood House.

A loud clang interrupted his progress. The workers froze in place, awaiting instructions. "System breech. System breech." A voice screeched through the air, barely louder than the clang. It was the signal, but Henry had to scurry to assume his assigned position. He wasn't ready for what happened next. Arrows flew from the far end of the room. Edward was in position. He was shooting his arrows with accurate precision. While he remained invisible, the trajectory of arrows did not.

"Ouch!"

"Hey!"

People dropped to the floor. Some moved, wrenched in pain.

Others did not as their life blood poured out of the hole created by the arrow. Cecil had managed to install some technological wizardry into Edward's arrows. The affect was devastating to watch. Henry counted. He knew how many arrows were in his son's arsenal. Twenty-four. It was the maximum a quiver could hold economically, allowing for ease in quick removal once the battle commenced.

The last arrow flew, felled a man at Henry's feet. The man continued to squirm. Henry raised his sword and put the victim out of his misery with one swift stroke. The sword glistened in the king's hand, but whether it was visible to others was a mystery. He swung again, claiming another victim.

"I have what we need," Henry heard Cecil's whisper. He pivoted away from the sound of the man's voice and swung his sword again, taking down another English technician. There were women in the room. He avoided them. He couldn't abide violence of any type against women. It was too much to expect him to raise a sword against a woman. His weapon obviously had a mind of its own. Good thing, too. As the king moved around, a woman held a weapon directed at him. Was he suddenly visible? It didn't matter. He had to do something. Fast. The sword took action, pulling Henry's arm up and slashing down, severing the hand bearing the threatened weapon.

The woman screamed. Henry resisted the urge to go to her rescue. To be a knight in shining armor. Another scream had diverted his attention. It was his son. "Edward." He moved towards the sound of the scream, the place where his son had been instructed to stand, from whence the arrows had flown.

"Father."

More people were flooding into the room. Weapons were being fired in every direction, seeking to claim the source of the invasion. Edward had lost his invisibility. He lay crumbled on the floor, blood oozing out of his chest where one of the modern weapons had found its target.

Henry moved closer, but he couldn't reach his son. The sword was swishing in every direction, carving a path of destruction. A sharp pain grazed his shoulder. He'd been shot. The impact would remove his ability to remain invisible.

"Take the boy," Cecil yelled from the other side of the room. "I have what we need. All is set."

He didn't have to explain further.

"Grab them!" An English voice shouted orders. "Don't let them escape. Block the travel device."

"It's not working, Sir," someone answered. Henry watched as a woman worked at a console across the long table. "It's been blocked, Sir." She glanced at the door where armed men and women continued to pour in. The woman shrieked and crumbled to the floor. Cecil had taken her down. His invisibility had also been compromised. Blood oozed from a wound to the arm. He quickly plugged something into the console, typed frantically, then stepped back and vanished. Henry didn't understand what Cecil had just done. All the instructions earlier about viruses and explosive devices was beyond his comprehension. His idea of explosives was a canon ball ejected from a canon. None of those were in use this day.

He didn't pause to think as he pushed his way through the remaining obstacles in his path and grabbed Edward. "Think of Stirling, son," he whispered and the two vanished as the room exploded in a plume of smoke and noise.

FORTY-THREE

Stirling Castle, May 1st, Year of Our Lord 1873

Henry watched as Edward opened his eyes slowly. Cecil had been and left, doing all he could to save the lad. The damage was too grave. There was nothing to do but wait for the final breath. Henry had not left his son's side since their return.

"Did it work?" Edward whispered in a breath, sounding choked, strangled.

"We did it, son." Henry nodded, forcing a smile through the wet cheeks where tears had streamed down unchecked. "The English scourge of the future has dissipated. We are safe. For now."

"For now and forever," Edward returned his father's smile. It was a weak smile, one filled with a wide myriad of emotions ranging from pain to sadness to joy. He gasped, his breathing becoming more raged. "Marry again, Father. Marry a Scottish lass. And call your first-born Robert."

"Even if it's a girl?" Henry tried to sound lighthearted in his banter, but it was hard. He felt his heart wrenching into a thousand pieces as he sat by his son, watching him die slowly.

"Then call her Robyn," Edward bantered back, his voice

barely audible. His breathing slowed. His hand, held tenderly by his father went limp. And he exhaled his last breath.

"No!" Henry sobbed, gathering the lifeless boy in his arms and hugging him tight. "No!"

He lost track of time. How long he knelt beside his son, cradling the boy's head in his arms, he didn't know. A knock on the door startled him from his mourning. He straightened himself, allowing Edward's head to rest once more on the pillow. He wiped the tear-stained cheeks and stood up slowly, making his way to the end of the bed, pulling the canopy drapes down as he circumnavigated the bed. He wasn't sure who was on the other side of the door, but he didn't want an audience to his son's passing. Not yet. Perhaps never.

Satisfied all was concealed, he cleared his throat and uttered a firm, "Enter."

George, his trusted confidante, best friend and man of all tasks, entered. "Your Majesty. I see you are up. Perhaps you would care to freshen up and change into something more formal. Queen Victoria and her son, the Prince of Wales, have arrived."

Henry was startled, a little confused. He rubbed his head. *What had Cecil said when they returned? Something about returning before. Before what? And where? The same place? No. Something didn't add up.* These chambers were at Stirling Castle. The last visit from Queen Victoria was at Holyrood House. Could this be an earlier visit?

"Along with the Princess Isabel," George added.

Yes, it was before the fateful last visit. Well before. It was the meeting with Isabel and the proposal which changed his life forever. Or had it changed it forever? Here he was being given a second chance. Would he make the same mistakes again? He rubbed his forehead with greater ferocity.

"Your Majesty." It was his attendant and sometimes friend. The man's voice was shadowed with concern.

"It's all right, George. Just a little headache. Give me a few minutes, then send in my valet."

"Very good, Your Majesty. I'll order some fresh tea, shall I?" He lifted his head towards the neglected tray of tea and sandwiches. When had it appeared?

"Yes. Take it away. Some fresh tea and toast would be fine. Make sure my royal cousins are shown to their chambers and have everything they need. I shall meet with them shortly."

"Yes, Your Majesty." George bowed, picked up the tray and exited the room, allowing the footman at the door to close it behind him.

Henry was alone again. "You weren't listening." He jumped at the sound of Cecil's voice.

Turning, he nodded towards the bed. "He's gone. My son is dead."

"Yes. He died a hero. Just as he wanted." Cecil made his way towards the king. "Now you have work to do in your time."

"Which is what?"

"May 1873."

"When I first meet Isabel and agreed to marry her. So, you really did mean 'before'. What has happened?"

"You returned to before Edward's birth, to a time when you could choose. Your clan chiefs, childhood friends, are all here, including Ian MacGregor's younger sister, Elizabeth, so named in honor of your mother, also Elizabeth. You always favored her growing up. But you were thwarted by the English queen, manipulated by your mother, and enticed by Isabel's fake charms. Now you know better. Now you can make a better choice."

"Elizabeth. Yes, I should marry her, shouldn't I?"

"It's your choice. But make it fast. My queen is restless. She has done her part, obliterating the implant and time travel program for all time. At your request. Or should I say command? Now, if you don't marry soon and produce an heir, she will no longer exist in my time."

Henry nodded. "Understood." He slapped Cecil fondly on the shoulders. "I suppose it means you don't exist either?"

Cecil nodded. "No. I wouldn't. And the English would have their way once again."

"If this implant program is obliterated, then how is it you are here?"

"I am the last and only one with the time travel ability. I'm here to take Edward. Well into the future. Even beyond my time. There I will perfect the program and keep it safe."

Henry felt around the back of his skull. "My implant is gone, isn't it?" Cecil nodded. "And I'll never see you again, nor Grandmothers Marie and Mary Elizabeth?"

"No. You will no longer have the ability to jump through time. Neither do they. Each of you must now live out your lives in the agreed upon time period. I won't return here, Henry. Never again. You are on your own. Be careful how you treat the English queen. Be careful how you reject Isabel. And live your life to its fullness. For yourself, for your descendants and for the people of Scotland."

"For now and forever." Henry gave his descendant a parting smile of understanding.

Cecil nodded. He moved towards the bed and gathered Edward into his arms.

Henry quickly moved in and gave his son one final kiss on the forehead. "Goodbye, my son."

FORTY-FOUR

"What do you mean, you can't marry me?" Isabel stomped her feet. After days of coyly trying to seduce the King of Scotland, she believed she had cast her net satisfactorily, entrapping the desired prey.

"The bands have been read." Henry didn't move from where he stood at the window, studying the gardens below and the people walking through them. Elizabeth was there, walking with her arm tucked into her brother's. As if sensing his eyes on her, she paused and glanced up to the window. A smile brightened her features. He returned it before turning away from the window. "I will marry Elizabeth MacGregor in three weeks, Isabel. I have made a promise and a commitment. I am not free to marry you. I never have been. I am terribly sorry if you feel you've been misled. Certainly not by me."

She stomped her foot again and screamed, her face scrunching up into a misery one only expected to see in a child undergoing a full-scale tantrum. "No!" She spat the word, spittle covering Henry's face. He stepped back. "You haven't heard the end of this." She stomped again before storming out of the room.

"I am quite sure I haven't." Henry pulled out a handkerchief and mopped the woman's spittle from his face. "It would appear I have dodged the bullet, in a manner of speaking," he muttered to himself. There was no one else in the room. His once, would-have-been bride-to-be had stormed out. "A twentieth century idiom my son shared with me. The son of a misguided union." Replacing his dampened cloth, he made his way to the door. He wanted to join his intended in the garden. Instead, the door slammed open as he approached and Edward marched in. Not his Edward. This one was older. This one was the Prince of Wales. Also known by those in his close circle as Bertie.

"What have you done to our cousin?" the prince demanded. "She's in a ripe mood now."

"I turned down her advances and refused to propose," Henry responded quite bluntly.

Bertie nodded as he paced the room. "Yes. I did hear rumors of bands being read in church, announcing your upcoming nuptials with some Scottish lass. So, it's true?"

Henry nodded, standing straighter with a sense of pride and ease. He was happy with his choice. Content. Elizabeth would make a fine wife, a wonderful, caring queen and a good mother of future Scottish rulers.

"Henry. Think sensibly. A union with Isabel would be much more beneficial than a union with some Scottish lass."

Before Henry could snap a response, the door banged open again and Queen Victoria glided in with purpose, anger evident on her face. "You have deceived me, Henry. You have deceived us all. I am disappointed in you. What do you mean, you're marrying someone other than our Isabel?"

"Exactly, Cousins." Henry chose to address both. "I firmly believe in keeping my interests, my country's interests, within my borders. Besides, I believe Elizabeth MacGregor is a better choice all around. She cares about my country and my people. Isabel does not."

"What does it matter about your people?" Bertie snorted, pausing only briefly from his frantic pacing, hands clasped behind his back. His pause was long enough to shoot a glare at his cousin. "You are the king. Not the people. You get to choose what's best for you, your country and your people. Not them." He pulled one hand from his behind-the-back clasp and waved it fashionably about to emphasize his point.

"Exactly, Bertie. It is my choice. And I choose Elizabeth."

"I suppose you love the girl." The queen, unlike her son, chose to stand, poised, hands clasped in front of her, as she glared at her opposition, a programed tactic, one she frequently used to unsettle her foe. It didn't work with Henry. Not any more. He was his own man, now. He knew how to stand his ground. He knew it was important for Scotland now and well into the future.

"Love. What does love have to do with anything?" Bertie shook his head in disbelief. "Marry for the country, do your duty and seek your pleasures elsewhere."

"Like you have? To my eternal disgrace?" Victoria quickly flashed a look of disgust at her son, before returning her attention to Henry. "Well? Do you, Henry? Do you love the girl?"

"Yes, actually. I do love Elizabeth." A blush crept up his neck as he glanced over the queen's shoulder and noticed Elizabeth standing in the doorway. He held out a hand, beckoning her in. "You, my cousin the Queen of England, should understand the importance and the power behind loving your partner. After all, didn't you love Albert?"

The queen visibly shuddered at the comparison, compressing her lips together in a firm scowl. She said nothing. Her gaze moved from Henry to the Scottish lass, as Bertie called her. Elizabeth's pace was slow. Calculated. Her eyes remained rivetted on her betrothed. Her king. She had heard his last words. He loved her. He had chosen her. She was honored. Yes. She loved him, too. Always had.

The moment was shattered when another figured barged into the room, shoving Elizabeth out of the way. "Move, trollop. How dare you block my entrance?" It was Isabel.

Henry moved to catch his intended before she fell flat on her face. "Isabel. This is uncalled for. I gave you no promises."

"You betrayed me!" She spat each word with punctuated exaggeration. "And for what? For this ..." she waved her hand viciously in Elizabeth's direction. "For this plaything of yours?"

"I would be careful, if I were you," Henry warned. "You are speaking to the future Queen of Scotland. In front of the King of Scotland. On Scottish soil, no less. You tread on dangerous waters, lady. Guard your mouth."

"He's right, Isabel." Bertie, ever the peacemaker, came to Henry's defense, albeit reluctantly. "This is not your place to protest. And not your right."

"But my child?" she whimpered.

Henry blanched. "What child? Are you pregnant, woman? Not by me. Definitely not by me."

"Isabel?" Victoria repositioned her pose and focused her attention on the raging woman. "Are you with child?" Isabel nodded. "Henry's?" The woman's eyes flittered back and forth between Henry and Bertie. Victoria cleared her throat. "You need say no more. You are a disgrace. And to think you would pass this unborn child off as Henry's." She tut-tutted. "Bertie. A word." Noticing his hesitation, she added more emphatically, "Now!" He followed his mother, like a puppy caught in a naughty act, his tail caught, dropping between his legs.

Victoria stopped abruptly at the door. "Isabel." The woman jumped. "You, too." The queen caught Henry's eye. "My apologies. It would appear my son had other ideas on how to put an

English lad on the Scottish throne. Not the way I would have planned it. We shall leave before the day is out." And she made her grand, sweeping exit.

A memory flashed through Henry's mind. The DNA test. In the future. He never did follow up. Didn't need to now. He knew the truth. Edward never was his. In so many ways, Edward would always be his.

Elizabeth stood beside her intended, the two now alone in the room. Henry walked over and shut the door. He took the woman in his arm and rubbed her back fondly, erasing the shudders shivering continuously along her spine.

"Henry. That woman. She was going to pass Bertie's child off as yours?" She shuddered again. "To be our heir, our next King of Scotland? I can't believe the audacity."

"Nor can I." Henry was quiet, thinking of his Edward. His son. In so many ways, he believed he was, but what had been revealed here, in this room, just moments before, added a dash of doubt in his thoughts. In more ways than one, he had definitely dodged the bullet.

"Are you sure I'm the best choice, Henry?" She pushed away all the while intently studying Henry's eyes, looking for reassurances.

"Yes, Elizabeth. You are definitely the one for me. And the one for Scotland." He lowered his lips to hers and relished in a feeling he had never felt with Isabel, past, present or future. This was definitely his choice.

EPILOGUE

Stirling Castle, Spring, Year of Our Lord 1879

Henry stood by the window and gazed into the courtyard below. His twin sons, Robert (the oldest by ten minutes) and Albert, now age four, were sparring with wooden swords, the sword master patiently guiding them through their paces. The boys weren't listening. They seldom did. They had minds of their own and enjoyed doing their own thing. The crack of wood and the shouts of childish banter was evidence enough.

"Father." Henry nearly jumped at the sound of the voice. He moved away from the window and glanced at the man who spoke. He thought he was alone. Obviously not. It was a rare privilege for a king to be left alone. Not as a father, either, as the boys were constantly seeking his attention. His praise. His encouragement.

"Edward?" Henry studied the young man standing before him. He shook his head in disbelief. "How is this possible?" He stood, rooted in place. Frozen. Unable to move. "You died in my arms. Six years ago. Yet, here you are, a young man of what? Twenty-five?"

"Twenty-seven, Father."

Rubbing his forehead, Henry continued to gape at this fine young man standing before him. He certainly didn't have the appearance of a Stuart. Not surprising, as he wasn't one. He had the look and air of Bertie at the same age. Bertie. The boy's real father. "How is this possible?" he repeated. "The implants were removed. Time travel expelled."

Edward chuckled. "You truly believe Cecil would give up entirely? No, Father. Cecil has been working on improvements. I'm his test subject. And, yes, I died in your arms. But, before the battle, Cecil ushered me into the future. Well into the future. The forty-fifth century to be exact. They have cures for my disease in the future. That's why I still live." He studied his father closely. "I wanted to see you again. I know, now, you're not my biological father. But you are my father in every other sense of the word."

Henry nodded, moving towards his son. Words escaped him as he pulled the young man into a fond embrace. Tears trickled down his cheeks. "Edward. My son." The men hugged. Henry was the first to pull away. "I did as you asked. I named my first born, Robert. He has a twin brother, Albert, after my mentor, Prince Albert."

Edward just nodded. "I know. I have all the history within my grasp."

Henry chuckled. "Yes, I guess you do. Then you probably know I have another son, still in the cradle. Only months old. I plan to christen him, Edward. After you. Edward Cecil. What do you think?"

"A fine name."

"So, what do you do in the fortieth century?"

"Forty-fifth century," Edward corrected. "I work with Cecil. I'm very good in the sciences, it would seem. Much like my grandfather, Prince Albert." Henry was jolted again with a startling realization: as Bertie's son, Edward was also the grandson of Queen Victoria and Prince Albert. Bertie did have a habit of getting himself embroiled in relationships with the opposite sex. And not always in his favor.

"Are you married? Children?"

Edward shook his head. "Not in the sense you would approve. It will be centuries before same sex marriages are both legal and morally accepted universally. And no children. I didn't want to pass on my genes and infect another generation of hemophiliacs."

"Who is he?" Henry tried to mask his shock and, given his era of living, his disgust. His own son. Well, not in the flesh and blood sense, but still Edward was his son. Married to a man. It was unconscionable. Rumors of English dalliances with the likes of Oscar Wilde, the Irish poet and playwright the English had long since claimed as their own, were big news items. But his son? Edward?

"Cecil?" Henry almost didn't hear him. Edward's voice was so soft.

"Cecil?" He exclaimed when the realization hit him full force. "He's old enough to be your..." He let the rest drop.

"I know," Edward chuckled softly. "In many ways, he is old enough to be my father, or, at times, my grandfather. And, you have to remember he was born centuries after my birth here in this timeline. But time travel has brought us together at a similar age. He's now only ten years my senior. We work together. We are so attuned to each other. There is no one else for me." Edward started to pace the room. "I didn't come to squabble over my choice in a partner. Cecil thought I should come. I have been begging to come visit for some time now. But Cecil didn't think it wise. Not until he had fine tuned a few more things with his device. We have more control now. It's safer and no one can steal it from us."

"Safer," Henry shook his head, a look of disbelief washing

across his face. He rubbed his brow and started pacing the room. "I don't believe for a moment it's safe. He was, and still is, tampering with people's lives. All across the time spectrum. It's not right, Edward. It's just not right."

Edward didn't answer right away. He moved to the window and watched the boys still dedicated to their swordplay. "I missed this, you know." He focussed his attention on the boys. "I never did get to play in the courtyard like they are doing now."

"You were brought up in the twenty-first century, Edward. Hardly a place for swordplay in a castle courtyard."

"True enough. It would have been nice to have this type of memory, though. A memory of this time to carry with me into the future." He sounded sad, in a way. Despondent, but also resigned to his fate.

"You could stay." Henry had ceased his pacing and joined the young man at the window. "It's your choice."

Edward shook his head. "No. My place is in the future. With Cecil."

"Cecil and his unconscionable time travel devices." Henry snorted, something he didn't normally do. "It's inhuman, you know. Goes against the flow of time and consequences. We all have our time in this world and we have to answer to what we do with our time when we reach the next world."

The young man stood silently, watching the boys, pondering the king's word. "Don't you want to know what happens to their future?" he finally asked. "The wars they'll have to face in the twentieth century. They're horrendous. Worse than anything the English witnessed in the Crimea or even the Boer War. You think Cecil is mad. Insane. You'll never get to see what madness and insanity can actually achieve. And all based on science. They'll create a device in the mid-twentieth century with the potential of wiping out this earth for all of eternity. And you don't want to stop it?"

"I can't, Edward." Henry placed a hand fondly on his son's shoulder. "And neither can you. Some things in life are just meant to be."

"So, if Cecil offers you another chance to try time travel, you'll refuse?" It was a question, one masking a tone of hopefulness in the young man's voice.

"I've made my choice, Edward. After our battles in the future, I chose to live out my life in this timeline. As did our ancestors, Grandmothers Marie and Mary Elizabeth, by the way. Cecil sent me to see how they were doing."

"And ask them the same question you're asking me now?" Edward nodded in response to his father's revelation. "And they gave you the same answer I'm giving you now?" He nodded again. "I've made my choice, Edward. And so have they."

Edward was silent. Henry sensed the boy had come to see him with high hopes. "I won't be seeing you again then, Father," he spoke in little more than a whisper, a catch in his voice revealing the anguish he was attempting to hold within. "You've made your choice and I've made mine."

"Life is all about choices, son. What happens after we make our choice is called consequence. I hope what you have seen in the future can be averted, but some things we can't change. Sometimes change isn't for the better." As he talked, he felt a void beneath the hand he had rested on his son's shoulder. Edward was gone.

The boys chose the moment to glance at the window where he stood. He wiped away a tear leaking from the corner of his eye and braved a smile. He waved and nodded his approval.

Henry had made his choice. Many choices, in fact. His choice to marry Elizabeth had been the best choice of all. Their sons were fine lads to lead Scotland into the twentieth century. These wars Edward predicted in the future, a future only he knew about, obviously from his studies of history up to the forty-fifth century. If they were as bad as he said they were, then it would at least keep England otherwise occupied and less interested in its northern neighbor. *Choices. Yes, life was all about choices.* Choices allowed time to pursue its natural course of events. For better or for worse. For now and forever.

ACKNOWLEDGMENTS

I don't know if I would be here today as an award-winning author if it hadn't been for the encouragement I received from family: my parents, my husband and, especially, my grandmother, Margaret Murray (Dickson) Downer (1902-1995). Gran, as we called her, shared with me a passion for reading and history, particularly Scottish history, royal history and, of course, the stories and facts which surrounded the ill-fated Mary Queen of Scots. This passion revealed itself in the first book of this series, "Queen Mary's Daughter". Gran and I frequently discussed the controversy over Scottish independence. Personally, I have always wondered at the wisdom of amalgamating Scotland with England. Certainly, history records multiple incidents of English brutality against the Scottish people. If, as "Queen Mary's Daughter" suggests, there was another heir and another timeline existed with a clearly free and independent Scotland, then why not continue the Scottish royal line and add a few more valiant monarchs determined to follow the ideals initiated by Queen Mary Elizabeth I of Scotland. King Henry was introduced at the end of "Queen Mary's Daughter" and my readers asked hopefully if his story would be told. So, here it is.

Special thanks to the efficient and thorough editors at Clean Reads for their help and support in seeing this book to its published form.

HISTORICAL NOTE

What if? "Queen Mary's Daughter" challenged the recorded history of Scotland, setting the parameters for an alternate history, one where Scotland remained free and independent, one where Scotland didn't suffer at the hands of the English. Taking notes of what happened in our known timeline, I manipulated the events, using time travel to make some things possible. Hence, Mary Elizabeth, daughter of Mary Queen of Scots. This first book set a precedent for the events that followed. A new line of Scottish monarchy evolved. And, another royal time traveler, King Henry I of Scotland, who appeared at the end of "Queen Mary's Daughter", set the stage for another battle with England, a battle with England's Queen Victoria and her wayward son, Crown Prince Albert Edward (or Bertie as his friends and family called him). Taking the history as we know it, and the alternate history of Queen Mary Elizabeth I, I mixed facts with fiction and science fiction to develop a whole new plot, a whole new series of 'what ifs' and a whole new challenge to keep Scotland free and independent.

Historical facts and dates are accurate, for the most part, except where some events are fantasised to fit into the new plot, the new timeline which included a Scottish king in the nineteenth century. Snippets are shared from the first book, allowing the new protagonist, King Henry, to do his time jumps both to the future and to the past.

Our known timeline includes Queen Victoria and her desire to rule the world as Empress, her frustrated son who desired more power than his mother would allow, and the passion the English monarchy had for the Scottish Highlands, including Balmoral Castle built by Prince Albert as their Scottish get-away.

There are other places, events and personages of interest. This is a story, a work of fiction, pure and simple. It is a story that continues what "Queen Mary's Daughter" began: it opens up a realm of possibilities. What if....

History has been written, but, if time travel exists, history will be re-written countless times. Perhaps, even as you read this, the timeline you thought you knew has already changed. Sit back and enjoy an infinite realm of possibilities. Perhaps in another time, another dimension, there is another plausibility, another historical timeline, one in which Scotland remains free and independent.

Emily-Jane Hills Orford

2019

ABOUT THE AUTHOR

An avid gardener, artist, musician and writer, **Emily-Jane Hills Orford** has fond memories and lots of stories that evolved from a childhood growing up in a haunted Victorian mansion. Told she had a 'vivid imagination', the author used this talent to create stories in her head to pass tedious hours while sick, waiting in a doctor's office, listening to a teacher drone on about something she already knew, or enduring the long, stuffy family car rides. The author lived her stories in her head, allowing her imagination to lead her into a different world, one of her own making. As the author grew up, these stories, imaginings and fantasies took to the written form and, over the years, she developed a reputation for telling a good story. Emily-Jane can now boast that she is an award-winning author of several books, including *Mrs. Murray's Hidden Treasure* (Telltale Publishing 2019), *Mrs. Murray's Ghost* (Telltale Publishing 2018), *Queen Mary's Daughter* (Clean Reads 2018), *Gerlinda* (CFA 2016) which received an Honorable Mention in the 2016 Readers' Favorite Book Awards, *To Be a Duke* (CFA 2014) which was named Finalist and Silver Medalist in the 2015 Next Generation Indie Book Awards and received an Honorable Mention in the 2015 Readers' Favorite Book Awards and several other books. A retired teacher of music and creative writing, she writes about the extra-ordinary in life and the fantasies of dreams combined with memories. For more information on the author, check out her website at: http://emilyjanebooks.ca